PRAISE FOR *ARTEMIS SPARKE AND THE SOUND SEEKERS BRIGADE*

"Warning: Artemis Sparke is pure energy! Equal parts ecologist, artist, scientist and historian, Art had me riding her tailwind on her mission to protect the delicate salt marsh of Long Island Sound. And, oh my, the stakes are high—environmentally and personally! Kenna's well-crafted debut is a timely gift."

- Leslie Connor, National Book Award finalist and author of *The Truth as Told by Mason Buttle* and *Anybody Here Seen Frenchie?*

"Featuring a strong and compassionate character, *Artemis Sparke and the Sound Seekers Brigade* is an engaging story about friendship, protecting nature, and speaking up for what's right even when it feels like no one will listen. Some helpful ghosts add layers of humor and mystery to this heartfelt novel."

- Lynne Kelly, author of *Song for a Whale*

"Kimberly Behre Kenna has written a terrific middle-grade novel that will inspire readers of all ages... This entertaining page-turner has unforgettable characters, family drama, ghosts and secrets, surprises and suspense, and, without being pedantic, illuminates the urgency of battling climate change. The world needs more role models like Artemis Sparke."

- Pamela Gray, screenwriter, *Conviction, Music of the Heart, A Walk on the Moon*

"A timely theme, nuanced characters, a story brushed with a touch of magic. Kids will love following the lead of environmentalist, Artemis, as this book is rich with opportunities for science investigations and experiments."

- Carol Wallach, CT recipient of the Presidential Award for Excellence in Mathematics and Science Teaching

"Birds love Artemis Sparke. Trees love her. Readers, too, will be captivated by this fiery, quirky, and determined twelve-year-old protector of salt marshes. Kimberly Behre Kenna's debut novel is lively, magical, and wise. An essential read for these times when the earth is in such urgent need of care and we are in such urgent need of hope."

- Ona Gritz, author of *August or Forever*

"A lovely tale full of pluck, passion, perseverance, and a dash of enchantment. A heartfelt adventure with a courageous young heroine determined to save her beloved salt marsh against daunting odds."

- Sandra Waugh, author of *Lark Rising* and The Adventures of the Flash Gang series

"Tapping into guidance from the marshland creatures—as well as some ghostly advisors with powerful wisdom to share—Artemis connects a whole team of activists to help fight a major decision. Artemis Sparke's compassion for others, her environmental concerns, her creative activism, and her powerful voice, will surely spark inspiration to work for change. Kimberly Behre Kenna has written a page-turning guidebook for the next generation of readers who are inheriting difficult environmental problems, but who—as this book reminds us—have the potential to learn from the past and to create lasting change."

- Diana Renn, author of *Trouble at Turtle Pond* and *Tokyo Heist*

ARTEMIS SPARKE AND THE SOUND SEEKERS BRIGADE

Kimberly Behre Kenna

Fitzroy Books

The other creatures with which we share this world have their rights too, but not speaking our language, they have no voice, no vote; it is our moral duty to take care of them.

—Roger Tory Peterson

1

Artemis Sparke stood at the tippy-top of Fiddlers Creek trail, scanning the area with her binoculars. The entire salt marsh spread out wide below her. What used to look like a brushed green carpet last month was now a patchy quilt of dry spots and droopy grasses. It was a June that resembled winter, all dreary and brown. Up until then, this Long Island Sound salt marsh behaved in predictable, quantifiable ways. Art's field notebook entries proved it.

She pointed her binoculars to the sky. "RT? You up there?" Nothing but a few blotches of clouds. Art used her T-shirt to clear the lenses and looked again. She elbowed her friend. "Do you see him anywhere, Warren?"

"Nope," he said, shielding his eyes from the sun.

Usually, RT circled around when Art visited, but that day she didn't spot him. Art refocused the binoculars and scanned again. Her hands trembled, and her vision blurred. "RT!" she called again. "Please tell me you're all right."

Silence.

Art stuffed the binoculars into her backpack. "Come on," she said, waving to Warren.

The two trudged down the trail toward RT's tree in the woods. The past couple of years, RT and his mate had chosen the wooded area along the salt marsh for nestbuilding. Usually, wood thrushes nest much deeper in the woods, but sometimes they're forced to find a perfect place somewhere else.

Grabbing on to a low branch, Art swung herself up, pulled into a standing position, and hugged the trunk. RT's nest, an open cup made of leaves and roots and mud, sat in the crook of a branch at her eye level. She peeked in.

Empty.

"Last time there were two bald babies in here. That was a little over a week ago. No way the chicks could fly off on their own yet," she said.

"You sure of that timeline? Maybe they're all out practicing," Warren replied.

Artemis jumped to the ground. "I'm sure," she said. "Help me search?"

"I thought we were biking to Sandpiper Park today."

Artemis begged him with her eyes.

"Art, this will be our third official ride on a state park trail for the Summer Cycle Challenge. We need to log nine more to be eligible for the giveaway. Summer doesn't last forever."

"Nothing lasts forever, Warren. I'm not giving up on winning a new bike, but right now I need to find RT."

"Okay then," he said. "First the birds, then the bike ride."

"Deal."

Artemis peeked under nearby bushes while Warren combed the area for feathers or clues that might point to foul play.

"Oh no!" Art held something shiny up to the sky and examined it.

"A BB gun pellet," Warren said.

They picked eight more out of the dirt. Art brushed them off and dropped them into her pocket with a sigh.

Warren nodded. "Not a good sign."

"These BBs could easily kill birds. And who knows what'd happen if they ate them?"

Honnnk! Honnnk!

On the trail below, a biker sped through a gaggle of geese, pedaling so furiously that in a couple of pumps he was bound to go airborne. Art dashed down the wooded path.

"Art! Wait up!" Warren tripped over tree roots trying to follow.

Just as Artemis set foot on the salt marsh trail, another biker raced by, knocking her back into the brush. Warren arrived just in time to see her field notebook fly out of her hands into the salt marsh muck, scuttling fiddler crabs back into their burrows.

Five feet away, the biker jammed on his brakes, and Art coughed as his rear tire cycloned dirt around her head and torso. Brett Barlow and his twin brother, Henry. She shook her fist at him, pointing to a sign on the pedestrian bridge. No Bikes Allowed.

Brett smirked and pushed off on his bike. "You don't know nothin', crazy girl!"

Art picked up a twig and flung it toward his back tire where it caught in the spokes. The bike lurched, and the boy caught himself before he fell. He glared at Artemis, pulled out the twig, and tossed it on the ground. He pointed at Warren. "Didn't know seventh graders hung out with babies who throw tantrums when they don't get their way. What a pity."

His words dissolved in the summer breeze as he sped off to catch up with his brother.

"What were you thinking?" Warren asked, as he helped her brush the mud off her field notebook. "You know those boys will just make it harder for you—us—when school starts again."

"I've survived this long." She looked up at Warren. "Thanks to you along the way."

"This isn't a first-grade fight on the kickball field. I can't hold my own against those two eighth graders." He wiped sweat from his face, made his way to the bridge, and sat on the edge, skinny legs dangling above the tide pools.

Art sat next to him. "RT warned me bad times were coming for the salt marsh. I won't just sit around and do nothing."

"But you can't do stuff like that! You talk about not harming wildlife, but you throw sticks at humans. Plus, it's embarrassing."

Art flipped open her notebook and pointed to that day's entries. "Here's what's embarrassing to me, Warren. Today, before you got here, I counted ten fiddler crabs in a five-minute period. Last summer, in the very same spot, I counted thirty-three crabs. I plotted out the observation area both times with pencils and string at dead low tide. A square, four feet by four feet, exactly five feet from the base of that evergreen tree." She pointed at a tree down the path. "These results are significant. I'm embarrassed to say people have taken fiddlers for granted. Nobody's paying attention. And they're disappearing."

Artemis pointed to another entry. "The number of egrets spotted within eight feet of either side of this bridge during a fifteen-minute period: there were six a year ago, but none today. And I don't remember the last time I saw a red-winged blackbird. They're usually all over the place." Art brushed a mosquito from her arm. "The only things increasing in number here are mosquitoes."

Art loved numbers. Answers to mathematical problems were either black or white. Predictable. A comfort. But she never expected to end up with pages of numbers that dwindled toward zero as fast as a leaky boat taking on water. "There's more to this salt marsh problem than the Barlow twins, Warren. But we do have to stop those boys."

Warren watched the water swirl beneath them as it headed into the Sound.

"We used to have fun biking or swimming or going out on the boat. Now all you want to do is hang out in the salt marsh. It's not working for me, Art." He stood and turned to go.

"Warren, we can still do fun stuff, just not right now."

"Let me know when you're ready, okay?" He walked off, kicking an acorn into the marsh.

"Can't you be ready for me sometimes?" she called.

"You don't hold up your end of the bargain, Art. It works both ways."

Warren shoved his hands into his pockets and picked up his pace. The slump of his shoulders made Art's eyes tear, but she knew what she had to do.

Art started home, picking up eighteen more BBs by the time she got to the end of the trail. "I'm sure it's not even legal to shoot BB guns in a preserve like this." She stopped near the salt marsh entrance to examine the thinning green leaves at the top of the amaranth plant. Two plants flanking it could barely breathe they were so shriveled.

"Don't you worry, in another month you'll have flowers." She brushed the delicate leaves with her fingers. "I think you're beautiful without them, but bees and butterflies adore them." The amaranth blushed and stood up taller, spreading her leaves a little wider. "You all are like family. Better than family. And I don't want to lose any of you." The amaranth swooned and drooped. Or maybe it was just the wind.

Art scanned the sky for RT one last time. Nothing but a blank blue canvas.

Finally, at the road, she burst into a run toward home, her footsteps the only sounds in a place that used to hum and buzz with life.

In her bedroom, Artemis rolled a BB between her fingers and punched numbers into her phone with her other hand. After three rings, a woman's voice answered, "Horizons police, is this an emergency?"

Dropping the BB into the pile on her bedspread, Art took a deep breath and cleared her throat. "Yes. Er, I mean, n-not that kind of emergency."

"Point please, miss. I get ten calls an hour in summer sometimes."

"Some boys tried to—well, I don't know if they actually d-did but—"

"Is this a true emergency, honey, because if so, you should be talking to—"

"It's a p-problem—" She put her hand on her throat. *Not now!*

"I'm sorry, I didn't get that."

Deep breath. "In the s-salt mar—" *Rats!*

Art scooped up the BBs and flung them down onto the oval braided rug where they scattered and settled into the grooves.

"What kind of joke is this?" the operator said. Art shook her head and clenched her teeth in frustration. "You know it's a crime to tie up the line when people with real problems might need police assistance. Goodbye."

But this *was* a real problem that would get even worse if she couldn't focus and speak right.

Dropping to her knees, Art rolled her hands hard over the BBs, wishing the rug would swallow them up. A few pellets stuck to her palms, and she brushed them away like bugs. Then she picked up each one and dropped them into her metal wastebasket with the blue hydrangeas painted on it. They pinged like rain on a tin roof. Art wrestled the window open, grabbed the basket, and held it over the sill, ready to fling the foul things away.

That's when she heard him. *But-but-but!*

"You're alive!" She searched the sky for RT, but he didn't appear.

Artemis knew this particular call, the one that thrushes used to claim their territory. Today, this was his urgent reminder that someone needed to rescue the salt marsh.

She pulled the wastebasket back inside and rolled the pellets around into a vortex, focusing her thoughts. BB pellets didn't belong on the lawn any more than they belonged in the salt marsh. She grabbed her report card from her desk and pulled it out of the envelope. Mostly Bs except for Language Arts. According to her teacher, Mrs. Smythe, her oral presentations "lacked vigor." She tossed the report card on the floor, poured the BBs into the empty envelope, tucked it shut, and labeled it *Crime Scene Evidence.*

2

Darling, this is divine," Art's mother said, as she helped herself to another spoonful of macaroni salad.

During the day, her mom worked as part of the housekeeping team at the Horizons Hotel. They lived in an apartment on the hotel's third floor. In the late afternoon, she took a break to eat with her daughter before starting her evening waitress shift. Artemis was in charge of cooking supper every day. It gave her lots of chances to practice everything Chef Paul had taught her in the Horizons Hotel kitchen.

"There's something different about this salad today. A new herb?" Her mother inspected her plate, touching here and there with her fork, as if the answer hid under a lettuce leaf or was wedged inside a cherry tomato.

Art threaded four macaroni onto her fork and popped them into her mouth. "Dill weed."

Her mom put her finger to her lips and shook her head. No talking with a mouthful. Table etiquette was a must in the Sparke kitchen. Artemis understood about acting all proper at a table in a fine dining restaurant, but why they had to fake it at their secondhand kitchen-wobbler she'd never know.

"Did you swim today?" Her mother crossed her legs, and her sandal dangled from her swaying foot.

"Nuh-uh." *Because I was busy with my real family. Trying to help them out.*

"Then what did you do? Tackle some of your summer reading?"

"A bit." Art stood and put her plate in the sink, turned on the water, and watched a few pieces of parsley whirl down the drain. "Good day to read outside."

"Oh, Artemis, you weren't in the salt marsh again. That

area's not conducive to studying. You need to focus on your schoolwork, not on birds." She ground some black pepper onto her salad with a vengeance.

"Birds are academic. Nature. Ecology. Right?"

"Stick to your middle-school curriculum. Don't be making up your own." She winked at her daughter. "Let's turn that C in Language Arts into an A this fall."

"Face it, Mom, I won't ever even get a B from Mrs. Smythe because I can't speak straight when I'm nervous. Oral presentations are the pits."

"Honey, one day you'll grow out of that nervousness and surprise them all."

"Well, I hope it happens soon. The Barlow twins nearly ran me over in the salt marsh today, and I think they were shooting BB guns at b-birds."

"Boys grow out of that kind of behavior," her mother said.

"We can't just wait, Mom! They're trying to k-kill living beings right now!" Art shoved her plate into the dishwasher, and it clattered against the silverware, knocking a knife to the floor. "You should call the p-police," she said.

"We don't want to waste the police's time on something as trivial as BB guns. They need to focus on hard crimes."

"K-killing isn't a crime?"

"You know what I'm trying to say." Her mother shook her head as she pressed her finger onto some stray grains of salt on the table, then stuck the finger in her mouth. "Speaking of crimes, our neighbor in the purple house complained again about the music on the hotel terrace. Said it kept her dog awake last night."

"So wanting to g-get a good night's sleep *is* a crime?"

"Marion Moonchaser has been a problem for years, ever since Harry started the renovations. It figures she's unappreciative of his efforts to keep things looking nice. Her and that horrendous front door, with the ridiculous, kaleidoscopic, whatever-it-is painted on it."

"It's abstract art. It's beautiful," Art said.

"Pfft," her mother said, waving her hand dismissively. "You'd think she'd have learned to shut her mouth after that whole town meeting debacle. Speaking out against the hotel in front of all the people who benefit from the revenue it brings in. Disgraceful. She's made herself into a pariah."

Art's cheeks burned as she cleared her mother's plate. "Hellander k-keeps adding rooms and expanding the parking lot. The hotel just gets b-bigger and louder and—"

"Enough with the drama, Artemis. Please. I'm exhausted, and I still have a shift to go."

"The only d-drama is you sticking up for your new boyfriend."

"He is not—"

"He is! I s-saw you and Hellander hugging and…and stuff. You and Dad aren't even divorced yet."

"It's *Mr.* Hellander to you. And let's stick with the issue at hand. Mrs. Moonchaser's claims are illogical. The Horizons Hotel can't get any bigger without falling into Long Island Sound."

Artemis put the empty macaroni box in the recycling bin and wedged the lemonade bottle beside it. "Exactly what I mean, Mom," she said, rolling her eyes.

Her mother stood and put both hands on the edge of the table. She leaned toward Artemis, her neck elongated like a dumbfounded turtle. "What did you say?"

"Nothing." Art picked out a diet soda can from the trash and tossed that in the recycling bin too.

"Artemis Sparke. This hotel is our livelihood. We need to support it in every way we can. That means not focusing on everything you perceive as negative." Her mother got up and headed for the door. "I'm off to work. You know where to find me if you need me." And she left.

Art poured soap into the dispenser, closed the dishwash-

er with a thunk, and hit the start button. As the machine
burped into action, Art pulled on her green hoodie. The sun
had dropped, and it could get chilly at dusk.

Artemis leaned over in the hotel lobby to adjust her sandal
strap. Next thing she knew—*BAM!*—she was spread-eagled
on the floor.

"Oh my! Artemis, dear, I'm so very starry, er, sorry." Mrs.
Moonchaser reached down for Art's hand. "My mind was on
another planet, and I didn't see you orbiting around."

"Thank you, Mrs. Moon—" Her neighbor's left ear
throbbed deep crimson, like the embers of a campfire.
Art read Mrs. Moonchaser's odd ear like a thermometer; it
forecast what kind of a day she was having. Today looked
troublesome.

Mrs. Moonchaser reached up and patted her silver curls
into place over her ears. "I'll just gravitate toward the front
desk. I have some dark matter to discuss with Harry. Stop by
tomorrow, why don't you, and say hello to Prisbrey."

"I need to talk to you about the salt marsh," Art whispered. "The Barlow boys."

"Later I'll want to hear every word, but right now I need
to bring Harry back down to earth." She spun around on her
heel and strode toward the reception area.

Mrs. Moonchaser chatted with Rita, the receptionist who
worked the front desk. Then Mr. Hellander appeared, his
whole body as rigid as a soldier ready for battle. Mrs. Moonchaser could barely see over the counter, so it didn't make for
a very fair match, but she held her head high as she looked
the man in the eye. She pointed to the beach, then put her
hands on her hips.

Mr. Hellander spoke. It was a whisper, or tried to be, but
Art heard every word he said. "Stay away from this hotel." He
turned back to Rita and started to discuss some paperwork.

Mrs. Moonchaser rapped the desk with her knuckles. "Excuse me, we're not done here."

He blinked fast but kept talking to Rita.

"Ignoring me will not make your problems go away, Harry." He closed his eyes, his hand tensing into a fist. "We can settle this if you'd just tune in," she admonished.

Harry Hellander opened his eyes, turned to Mrs. Moonchaser, and pulled out his phone. "I asked you to leave. You continue to harass me, so I will call the police." Art moved closer to the desk, standing tall beside her neighbor. "And you, young lady, need to mind your own business," he said. "Be careful who you choose to stand with." He flicked on his phone and nodded at Mrs. Moonchaser. "She's trouble."

Art reached for his arm. "You c-can't—"

He pulled away before Art could make contact. "I most certainly can." He punched numbers on his phone.

"Wait!" Art said. Mr. Hellander waved her away. She cleared her throat. "P-please—"

Her words welled up, stuck, and she knew better than to keep trying to talk. Art blinked hard and looked at the ceiling, as if the solution to everything perched on the dangling light fixture. Mrs. Moonchaser put her arm around Art and led her away. "Come on, we'll pursue this matter another time," she said.

Mr. Hellander glared at them and put his phone back in his pocket.

Outside, Artemis and her neighbor stood by the bench at the front entrance. A plaque on the bench explained how the hotel had once been a private residence built in the 1800s, the Muiriel family estate. Art ran her fingers over the engraved letters. "He can't t-treat you that way," she said.

"He may come around. For now, your job is to keep on shining." Then Mrs. Moonchaser hobbled down the porch steps and headed toward her home.

Shining? I doubt it. I'm only twelve, and I already feel burnt out.

3

Dusk snuck up like a secret, thanks to a shroud of clouds. Streetlights would soon eclipse the beach, and the outdoor hotel crowd would smother another peaceful night.

The heat from the cars seared Art's bare skin as she traipsed through the packed parking lot. Nobody else seemed bothered by the things that bothered her. Maybe Brett Barlow was right. Maybe she was crazy.

She pulled her bicycle out of the storage shed. Today was definitely a triple-loop day. By the time she biked down West Wind Road, turned left on Surf Side Place, then back to the hotel—and did this three times over—she'd feel better. Whizzing along the seaside roads washed worry from her brain.

Artemis adjusted the bungee cord snug around the plastic milk crate that was fastened to her handlebars, then she hopped on and pedaled away.

Mr. Hellander's the disgrace, not Mrs. Moonchaser. Okay, yeah, if it weren't for Mr. Hellander and his hotel, we wouldn't have food on our table or a place to live. But that doesn't mean Mom should go ahead and fall in love with the guy.

Even a quality bike ride couldn't erase the jumbled thoughts in her head that day.

She stood and pumped her bike up the last bit of hill, anticipating the thrill of zooming down the other side.

As she coasted, dark clouds drifted in, and Art's eyes twitched as she tried to focus. It was like looking through wax paper, all muffled and misty. Just like her family. With her dad not living with them anymore, life was changing shape, and the shifts felt dizzying. Luckily, her salt marsh family had slipped into place nicely and up till now had stood sturdy. When Art looked into the eyes of the wood thrush or chipmunk, she saw her own reflection. They all spoke different languages but still understood each other just fine. Now her salt marsh family was shifting, and Artemis couldn't stand losing it too.

Art screeched to a stop and scanned the beach. "Rats. Here we go again." She unhitched the crate and trudged over the sand to the water's edge. "Four more plastic cups to add to the collection." Each cup was decorated with an orange sun setting over turquoise water. The Horizons Hotel logo. "How embarrassing." She dropped them in the crate, along with a red plastic comb and three chunks of a chewed-up buoy, then returned to her bike.

As Art rounded the bend, completing her third loop, a flare of yellow-green light in the brush caught her eye. Fireflies! The top of the bush blazed like a birthday cake with a billion candles. She couldn't remember ever seeing such a brilliant display, especially this early in the evening. Finally, an increase in numbers for her field notebook. Estimated, of course. On second thought, estimation was not very scientific, so she stopped and took six pictures of them with her cell phone.

After her ride was done, Art stashed her bike back in the hotel shed and pulled her journal out of her backpack. Then she scrolled her phone for the photos.

Where were they?

Art closed her eyes and conjured up the flaming bush and, breathing deeply, she counted to ten. Then she looked again for the pictures. Nothing.

Am I crazy? No. Those fireflies were real.

Art plopped down on the grass, cupped her hands to her mouth, and called, "Ee-oh-lay. Ee-oh-lay"—the middle part of a wood thrush's three-part song. Musical and flute-like, the wood thrush's songs were Art's favorites.

RT's silhouette soared against the dusky drape of evening sky, and he lit on a branch just inside the small wooded area bordering the hotel. Finally!

RT and Art went way back, to the day she and her father hiked the woods by the salt marsh and stopped to eat cream cheese and jelly sandwiches at the base of an oak tree. RT sat on a branch above, looking down. He cocked his head and nodded his beak at her. Very unusual, as this species of bird was quite shy and preferred to stay hidden. The wood thrush's cinnamon-brown upper body provided good camouflage when foraging in leaves or even when sitting on a branch. Art nodded back, careful not to let her father see. He thought she was too wrapped up in animals and plants and not enough with humans.

Since then, Artemis visited RT, named after Roger Tory Peterson, the famous bird-guide author, almost every day. RT was quickly becoming her new best friend, seeing as Warren, her best human friend, was as unpredictable as New England weather in October. Warren had grown quieter, too, but maybe that was because of what was going on with his dad.

Ee-oh-lay! Ee-oh-lay! RT tweeted.

She squinted into the deepening night. "RT, you warned me to pay attention, but this is much worse than I expected."

Bup-bup-bup! His distress call came again.

She stood. "I know. But why is your nest empty? Are you and the babies okay?"

The bird's pitch rose higher, and he sang faster. "Pit-pit, pit-pit, pit-pit!" When RT first sang to her in that sharp, mournful tone, she learned it meant caution.

Pit-pit-pit! sounded over and over like a machine gun.

She walked to the tree. "RT, I'm not sure how to help."

Then RT trilled something new, a bewitching melody unique to his species, thanks to their two-section voice box. Two different strands of notes harmonized with each other, weaving in and out like the pink clematis on the front fence. She envied his easy voice, and that night his tune swept over her and settled deep in her bones like a warm bath. It was as if he wanted to leave her with a gift despite his bleak warning. Then, RT flitted from the branch and disappeared into the thicket. Just like that.

"Oh no, you don't!" Artemis rushed to the thicket and shone her phone flashlight into the dark brush. "Where'd you go, silly bird? I've been looking all over for you."

She gently drew the branches apart, but she couldn't see him anywhere.

Things changed fast. RT's disappearing act was evidence of that, along with the missing photos of the fireflies on her phone and the coming and going of Mrs. Moonchaser's pink ear.

Art went back to her bike, unhitched the crate, and carried it to the hotel kitchen.

"Hey, Artemis! How goes it?" Chef Paul said as he wiped down the counters. "You're just in time to help with prep!"

His daughter, Jess, looked up from the sink where several spatulas floated in a soapy bath. "Yeah, Art, the garden-club lunch is tomorrow. I could use some help making veggie dips."

"I'd love to help, but I'm just dropping off some recyclables, and then I have a few things I need to take care of. But I'll try to get here later," Art said as she opened the closet door.

Chef Paul tossed his rag in the linen basket. "That closet's just about bursting. You sure you don't want to send some of it over to the transfer station?"

Artemis sorted her new finds into the bins according to

color. "Nope. I'll be down to scrub this stuff, hopefully to-morrow. Then I'll get them out of here."

Jess shook one of the bins to settle the items and make more room. "Your mom doesn't mind all this trash in your apartment?"

"I sort the things I want to keep in shoe boxes in my closet. She doesn't even see them. Soon I'll be using them for an art project, so it won't be an issue."

Jess nodded. "I can't wait to see what you make this time. Mind if I take pictures of you at work?"

Art gave a deep bow. "I'd be honored. Your Ansel Adams presentation at the fifth-grade open house was the most popular exhibit."

Jess blushed and adjusted her glasses on her nose.

Artemis picked up the empty crate and headed out. "I'll let you know when I start the project. I have a feeling this piece is going to be an important one."

"Fun!" Jess said.

Back in her room, Artemis sketched the firefly bush in her field notebook and added a paragraph about the photos disappearing, wondering if she'd deleted them by mistake. Facts were important, and she needed to record each and every one in order to build a persuasive argument. All facts should be backed up with numbers whenever possible. After all, numbers equaled truth.

Art's hypothesis was that there was an inverse relationship between the number of BBs and the number of creatures still living in the marsh. And there seemed to be a direct relationship between the increase in hotel business and the increase in trash on the beach. But she needed to collect more data before reaching any conclusions.

Art sketched the beach roses, decorating them with down-turned eyes and frowning petals. Below the roses she drew the egrets, their feathers hanging limp and dingy from their wings, like becalmed sails. All evidence and clues needed thorough and clear representation.

Recordings complete, she stared at the page, gripping her pencil until it hurt to think. *Snap!* The pencil broke in two. Artemis examined the ragged edges. *Was it really even possible for a kid to fix something so broken?*

The salt marsh and its neighboring woods had taken care of Artemis for years. Now it was her turn to take care of them. If Mrs. Moonchaser was right and the hotel was a part of the problem, she'd have to be careful of what she said or did. Sometimes her anger got a bit out of control. And right now, she was fuming.

4

The slant of the morning sun made the figure on the dock look like a cardboard cutout. But even from a distance, the lanky silhouette, with his shoulder blades jutting out like wings sprouting from his back, was unmistakable. Every time Warren cast his rod, the right wing popped up and then disappeared. He had a habit of shucking his hair out of his eyes by tossing his head back and blowing up at his forehead at the same time. Every so often he'd shift from one foot to the other, as if the dock was too hot for two feet at once.

"Hello, Warren." Art sat and dangled her legs over the edge of the dock.

"Hey, Art. How ya doin'?"

Before she could answer, the metal bucket next to his grandfather's old tackle box jiggled and thumped.

"Flounder?" she asked, nodding toward the bucket.

He nodded. "It's been weeks since I caught a fish." He cast his line again, and the bobber made a satisfying plop in the water. "Maybe they're all on summer vacation too."

"The answer's probably more complicated than that. But you'll eat what you catch, right?"

"You know I do, Art. This'll be lunch. Plus, I'm nowhere near the state limit of four a day."

"Let's keep track of how many fish you catch this month so we can compare it to last summer at this time. I'll add the info to my field notebook. Just record the days you fish, the weather, and the number of fish you catch," she said. "Okay?"

"Mm-hm."

Wow. Not exactly enthusiastic.

Warren reeled in his line to check the bait. The sandworm dangled from the hook. He cast it out again, and then he held the fishing pole out to her. "Here, wanna give it a go?"

Art glared at him.

Warren shrugged and cast his line again. "You have that chilly look you been gettin' a lot these days, Art."

Art stood and put her hands on her hips. "Not chilly. Worried. Worried that you're not interested in why you haven't been seeing m-many fish around this summer."

"Believe me, it's not worth it to worry about stuff you can't change."

"Maybe I *can* change some things."

Not the hotel scene though. Art was reminded of that daily as she observed summer unfolding as predictably as the tides. Calypso music spilled from speakers on the beach. Lawn mowers left green stripes in their wake as they whirred across the property. Lifeguards revved up jet skis, readying them for rental.

A sunburned boy in a Horizons Soccer shirt argued with Lenny, the lifeguard.

"Sorry, kid, you got to be sixteen and have a certificate for operation of one of these things. It's the law," Lenny said.

"Come on, Len, just this once," the boy pleaded.

"Warren!" Art pointed at the boy. "It's Henry Barlow!"

"Figures," Warren said.

Henry skulked to his bike and took off. He rounded the corner of the parking lot so close that a mom pushing a baby carriage had to step into the garden to avoid him.

"Geeze," Artemis said. "Barlow should have his bike taken away."

"Got another one!" Warren reeled in the line frantically, his eyes shining with expectation. He eased the hook out of the squirming fish's mouth and dropped it in the bucket. "Total's up to two." He gave Art a thumbs-up, secured the hook end of the line to the rod's handle, and grabbed his bucket. He turned around and started down the dock toward the beach.

Art looked down. "Hey! You forgot this." She caught up with him and handed him his Yankees cap. Warren set down the bucket and stuffed the cap into his back pocket. As he reached for his bucket, his shirt came untucked, exposing a raw gash on his lower back. Art stopped short. "What happened?" she asked. Warren kept walking. "War, your b-back. It's all red and—"

He put the bucket in the other hand and struggled to tuck the shirt back in. "It's nothin'."

"Come on. You can t-tell me, Warren."

"One a those things you can't do anything about," he said.

"But maybe together we can."

He tugged his baseball cap on, pulling it low over his eyes.

"Does your mom know?" she asked.

"Not sure, but she and my father fight enough these days as it is." Warren sauntered ahead of her, his strides long and resolute.

She picked up her pace. "Your dad d-drinking again?"

Warren nodded.

Art stopped and watched as he walked away. "Sorry," she called out. He shrugged and kept walking. When Warren went silent, nothing could get him to speak before he was ready. His father had that effect on him.

"War, if you want, we can do that bike ride at Sandpiper Park later on. Let me know."

"Right-o," he called back.

Art grabbed her rake and bucket from the shed and headed for the salt marsh. She raked till her shoulders burned, wishing she could do away with mean fathers along with the cigarette butts, candy wrappers, and deflated balloons tangled up in the cordgrass. Plastics went in a separate bag to add to her collection in her closet. Soon enough she'd have plenty of colors to choose from to create something spectacular. But Artemis wasn't the only one working hard that morning.

A girl in cutoff sweatpants and a yellow tank top dragged a tarp down a hill toward the east end of the salt marsh. The house on the hilltop overlooked a lawn that unfurled in a seamless green cascade. When the girl got to the marsh, she opened the tarp and shook it out.

"Great. Karla the kickball queen makes her own rules on and off the field." Art dropped her rake and whispered to the cordgrass, "I'll be back to finish combing this garbage out of you in just a minute."

Art stood and waved her arms at Karla, but she kept shaking grass clippings into the lower salt marsh. Artemis moved closer. Clippings clumped up around the base of the sea grass. Art knelt down and gathered them into a pile.

Karla sneered at Artemis. "What is your problem?"

Art swallowed and took a breath. "Nitrogen. It c-can…" *Focus.* "It can b-be a…"

"Nitrogen schmitrogen. Don't worry about it. They're just grass clippings. My father has me do this every summer."

Art's teeth clenched and she took another step toward Karla, holding her arms out in a wide blockade, but the girl pushed past. Art grabbed the corner of the tarp and yanked, but not before Karla dumped the rest of the clippings into the salt marsh.

"Stop being a pest," Karla said. "I'm just trying to get some work done." Then she folded the tarp, tucked it under her arm, and went back up the hill.

Before Karla even disappeared inside her house, Art began to gather up the clippings. She wasn't about to let the cordgrass here end up like the grass on the other side of the marsh.

"If you sit in this mess, at first you'll get greener, but soon you'll have less energy for your roots. You'll get skinny and bent over like little old men. Then, before you know it, that obnoxious Phragmite reed will take over and choke out the native plants that are homes for all kinds of creatures."

Artemis managed to clear away a small mound of clippings, but there looked to be a mountain's worth left. "This'll take more effort than I thought." She scowled at Karla's house, picked up her bucket and rake, and headed back home.

5

Before Artemis got a chance to rap on her neighbor's door, barks from inside announced her arrival. Mrs. Moonchaser appeared, her apron smudged orange and green, her curls tucked into a paisley scarf.

"I was beginning to wonder if you'd fallen off the face of the earth." She hugged Artemis, and Prisbrey jumped up for pats. "Come. I just finished juicing."

Art followed her to the kitchen, past Simon, a tall metallic sculpture, standing in the corner of the foyer. His index finger rested on his chin, and the Horizons Sentinel was tucked under his arm. A Moonchaser masterpiece. Using pliers, scissors, and a glue gun, she transformed soda cans, cardboard, and other castoffs into works of art which had inspired Artemis to create her own. Mrs. Moonchaser loved to dress up Simon every so often, hanging candy canes from his fingers in December, and hooking a basket of chocolate hearts over his arm in February. Today the sun shone down through the skylight onto Simon, spotlighting a man contemplating the problems of the day.

In the kitchen, Art cleared away empty soup cans to make space at the table. She watched Mrs. Moonchaser pour a frothy dark liquid from a stainless-steel pitcher into two glasses. Art took a sip and the tart tang of kale—or was it basil?—made her lips smack.

Mrs. Moonchaser handed her a small blue bottle. "Found it in the Hansens' recycling bin."

Art ran her finger over the opening. "Smooth. Thanks. I don't have many blue ones in my collection."

"Summer must be keeping you busy. It's been almost a week."

"A lot's happening, so fast that—" Art gasped, catching sight of Mrs. Moonchaser's ear, which had erupted in scarlet splotches.

Mrs. Moonchaser pulled on her ear lobe and sat. "I know. It's been flushing a lot lately."

"Sorry, I didn't mean to stare," Art said.

"No apology necessary. Few people notice. You're an observer, like me."

"Lately, your ear's been brighter, redder."

"Some days it's more obvious than others. I go into hyper-listening mode when I hear something, and I'm not quite sure what to make of it. Trying to detect undercurrents." She leaned forward and whispered, "Subtext."

"Subtext?"

Prisbrey's legs twitched. Maybe she was dreaming about a good cat chase.

"What a person's really saying but doesn't say aloud," Mrs. Moonchaser said.

"Awesomazing! Like ESP."

"Nothing extraordinary that any person can't access. If they detach and come up for a breath, that is." Mrs. Moonchaser stripped the label off a pea soup can and slid two other cans over to Artemis. "Consider your own father."

Artemis picked at a tomato soup label. "What about him?"

"My point is, I only see him walking to and from his office. I never see him outdoors hiking or birdwatching anymore."

Art shrugged. "He's really busy with work. Besides teaching at the university, he's writing a book."

Mrs. Moonchaser shook her head. "You and me, we're observers, a vanishing breed."

Art arranged the bare cans into a straight line. "What do you mean?"

"I'm afraid it's only natural to go from disregarding nature to disregarding humans."

"There've got to be others like us that care about nature. I just don't know a lot of them yet," Art said.

"Now there's a nice shot of optimism. Correct you are, we certainly aren't alone."

Artemis pulled a book from the shelf. *Horizons, Then and Now.* She leafed through the pages until she came to some photos. "I've read the copy you gave us when we moved here, at least a zillion times, Mrs. Moonchaser."

"The book's a classic. A beauty."

Art pointed to old photos of lush gardens, and a yard that stretched almost to the beach. "It's hard to believe the hotel property used to look like this."

Pink beach roses tumbled over a stone wall, and black-eyed Susans popped up in patches all over the property. There were three buildings—a big blue house with white shutters and a wraparound porch, a yellow guest cottage that looked like a gingerbread house, and a garage with cedar shakes weathered to a muted gray. A gull perched on the steep roof.

"I wonder what the Muiriel family would think about their property being turned into a hotel," Art said. "Tennis courts instead of gardens. A brick barbeque terrace where the guest house was. And where are all the stone walls?"

Mrs. Moonchaser stood and looked over Art's shoulder. "Muiriel handed the property down to Mr. Hellander's great uncle. With Harry now at the helm, we're lucky the integrity of the main home was maintained when they remodeled."

"I know. The old stuff is the reason I love the hotel so much. Like how the rooms don't follow each other in a line down the hall. They're scattered around. And how every guest room still has a name plate above the door that match-es what it looks like inside."

"Family must've been nature lovers themselves," Mrs. Moonchaser mused. "Edelweiss for a bedroom painted rose, and the Morning Glory, all sapphire blue."

"The Honeysuckle Room's my favorite. The walls remind me of butter melting on a baked potato. They're creamy, almost. Time goes so fast when I help Mom clean the rooms because I make up stories in my head about who lived there hundreds of years ago." Art flipped ahead a few more pages. "What do you think of this bit about ghost sightings?"

"Absolutely true. There are a million stories in those old walls, and I bet there are plenty of ghosts hovering around waiting to tell them."

Artemis gathered up the soup-can labels. "I'd totally like to meet one. I wonder if there's a special way to call for a ghost."

"Good question."

"If people's spirits are still hanging around after death, they must have a reason for being here, don't you think?" Art finished her smoothie and put the glass in the sink.

"I do."

"Like the ghosts in that Christmas movie."

"*A Christmas Carol.*"

"That's the one. Those ghosts had a mission to teach Scrooge some things. I'd love to get some smart ghosts to help me with my mission."

"Mission?"

"Yeah, you know, the salt marsh. Two boys on bikes were shooting BBs there the other day."

"So how does one protect the salt marsh from bands of boys with bad motives?"

"That's what I'm working on. There's more behind that sick salt marsh than the boys, though. Like the hotel expansion, and people tossing trash and grass cuttings in the wrong places."

Art put the labels in a basket of odds and ends that Mrs. Moonchaser was saving for a future project. "I suppose I could try to talk to people, you know, explain why the town needs the salt marsh to stay healthy." She stopped and looked at her neighbor. "Forget that. Sometimes I get so mad that words don't come out at all."

"Nothing wrong with anger. Just channel that energy into something more useful."

Mrs. Moonchaser made it sound so easy, like loading left-over vegetables into the food processor and turning them into soup.

"Try observing and then extrapolating," she said.

Art pulled out her field notebook and flipped to the first page. "I have been observing. Just like RT told me to. It's all right here." She handed Mrs. Moonchaser the book and watched as she skimmed through the notes, her eyebrows lifting and falling like a cormorant's wings.

She closed the field notebook and handed it back to Art. "Facts are useful and these are pretty clear." She patted the cover.

"But what good will this do if nobody reads it?" Art asked. A breeze blew in through the window, ruffling the *Horizons Sentinel* newspaper in the crook of Simon's metal arm and finally flipping it to the ground. Art picked it up and put it back in place. "It's not like I can publish my field notebook and expect people to read it with their morning coffee."

Mrs. Moonchaser stood and contemplated the empty cans on the table. "You never know what's possible."

"Wait!" Artemis grabbed the newspaper from Simon. "But I could write a letter to the editor of the *Sentinel* about what I've observed." Art slumped to the floor, her back against the wall. "Nope. My mom would kill me." She popped back up. "But I could write an anonymous letter!"

"That's a good start. Trust your numbers and believe in yourself." Mrs. Moonchaser pointed to Simon. "Take Simon Rodia, for instance. He spoke very little English but managed to bring pride to his neighborhood by building the Watts

Towers using all recycled objects. After work and at night, no less!"

"It sounds unreal, like a fairy tale," said Artemis, staring at Simon.

"It's the truth. Go read some books about him. And rumor has it that Rodia once visited the Horizons Hotel back when it was the Muiriel Estate."

"Maybe Mr. Rodia's the ghost that people saw wandering around the hotel."

"Maybe."

Art's arms and back tingled. "A bit creepy, but I'd give anything to meet that guy and hear his stories." She pointed at the sculpture. "Was he really that tall?"

"Doubtful. I suppose I think of him as a man of stature because of his persistence and passion. He worked for thirty-four years building the Watts towers, one of which is 99 1/2 feet tall."

Prisbrey got up and put her head on Mrs. Moonchaser's lap. "Okay, then," she said. "Time to go, my friend. You've got work to do, and I've got to give Prisbrey a pedicure. We'll touch base in a few days."

Prisbrey followed Mrs. Moonchaser out of the kitchen, her nails tick-ticking on the wood floor. Art pulled the front door closed behind her, but not before she gave Simon a quick wave. The sun winked off his tin-can face.

It gave her the heebie-jeebies. Hopefully it was a friendly wink.

6

Horizons Hotel was fully booked that week, as usual, but an unusual number of couples wanted extra cots in their rooms to accommodate young children. Artemis received a small paycheck for helping her mom out with housekeeping during busy times.

"I heard from your dad," Art's mom said, as she plumped the pillows. "He's been traveling in Greece to—and I quote—immerse himself in the culture he teaches and gather information for his book. Unquote."

Art's shoulders stung from raking, and she winced as she tugged a fitted king sheet onto the bed. "He's visiting ancient ruins?"

"Some things never change. His obsession with the past nearly took over our entire home."

"Tell me about it. I nearly killed myself climbing over antique urns and statues of Greek gods to get to my bike in the back of the garage. Some cool stuff, though," Art conceded.

Her mother gathered up the dirty bathroom towels, her sneakers squeaking on the tile floor. "Fill up that pail, and I'll go grab a mop. This bathroom floor is sticky with hair spray."

Art put a bucket under the tub faucet, turned on the hot water, and sat back on her heels. The pipes grumbled and groaned but no water came out. Sometimes, in old buildings like these, it could take a while.

"Okay." Artemis looked all around. "All clear. I've got to start somewhere, and this room's as good as any."

"Mr. Rodia?" she whispered, looking up at the ceiling. "If you're around, I wouldn't mind having a little chat."

Silence. And the bucket was still empty. Art turned the hot water handle the other way. "Come on now."

The hotel was as quirky as a dear old grandpa. It required patience and kindness, and the result was a wonderful friendship. Mr. Hellander considered creaks and grunts a nuisance, and he insisted on replacing anything that revealed its old age. He didn't understand that new things just didn't carry magic like the old.

Still no hot water. Art turned the cold water on. It spurted out in gushes, rushing into the bucket and spraying everything nearby with a fine mist. "Balance. We could use a little balance," she said as she turned down the cold and eased the hot back on. "Ah. Now that's more like it."

As the bucket filled, Art imagined the big bathroom as a study or a sewing room or a child's bedroom back in the old days. Maybe Mr. Rodia had used the room to sketch out plans for a nursery, seeing as he had a knack for building and all.

"Yoo-hoo? Mr. Rodia?"

Whoosh!

The bucket overflowed, and she twisted the faucet off. The water circled and eddied in the bottom of the tub and then disappeared except for a small puddle that remained stagnant. Art brushed at the water, trying to move it along, but it wouldn't budge. A deep croaky sound spurted up through the drain, and a stream of water shot out. Art jumped back. It gurgled and spat again.

She knelt and ran her hand over the water, as if comforting a stray kitten. "Okay, okay. I'm listening now." The water slowly began its descent down the drain again. Now it tripped and trilled like a song sparrow.

"What are you trying to say?" She turned on the hot water, just allowing a small stream to flow out. She let it run over her hand and through her fingers in glistening, snaky tendrils that landed and drained smoothly. But then she heard something else.

It was a sound straining to be heard, a muffled echo kind of thing. She turned off the water, knelt, and spoke toward the drain.

"Please, Mr. Rodia, I'm a friend of Marion Moonchaser's. Can we talk?" A gurgle, and then the water chugged down the drain—all of it—leaving the tub blank and quiet. She looked up under the shower head and down into the drain. Nothing.

"Drat," she said. "Just forget I even asked."

Then, like steam from a tea kettle, a misty figure slid out of the drain and hovered above the tub. Finally! Mr. Rodia had heard her.

But he hadn't.

It was a woman. A shawl of deep orange with bright yellow swirls draped her shoulders, and a mass of long brown braids were gathered in a bun at the nape of her neck.

"Whoa!" Art gasped, stepping away from the tub. The woman sparkled, not like a diamond, but softer, like the autumn sun's reflection on Long Island Sound in the late afternoon. She smelled like fresh linens, delicate yet durable. Art edged closer and the woman's face began to clear. Her smile looked familiar. Just when Art was close enough to reach out and touch her, the woman dissolved down the drain with a gentle hiss. Or maybe she was saying *shhhh!*

Art knelt and gripped the edge of the tub. "Come back!" she pleaded.

"Artemis!" Her mother stopped short as though she'd hit a wall. "Who were you talking to?"

"N-nobody." Art drizzled some special soap into the bucket, took the mop from her mom, and stirred the water into a froth. In secret, she'd swapped out the chemical-laden soap and refilled the bottles with green soap. This is where earning money came in handy. Mr. Hellander claimed the eco-friendly soap cost too much.

"I distinctly heard you speaking. You asked someone to come back." Her mother removed the dirty towels from the rack and replaced them with two fresh ones, spacing them apart just right. "Remember the rule about phones during work hours."

Art stabbed the mop back and forth across the floor. "The water just t-took a while to come on." Ghosts didn't fit into her mom's idea of sanity.

"You were talking to the water, Artemis?" her mother demanded, her lips pursed in disapproval.

"No big d-deal. A little malfunction."

"No big deal? Harry needs to know when things need repair. His—our—livelihoods depend upon it." Her mother jerked the tub faucets on, and they responded appropriately. "There's nothing wrong with these pipes. On second thought, don't say anything to him about the plumbing. No sense in riling him up over nothing."

Glug-a-glug-a-glug. Art glanced at the tub drain and winced. But her mother was busy scrubbing the sink as if bacteria were engrained in the porcelain. When she turned on the hot water to rinse it, the water streamed out fast and hard. She fumbled to turn it off. "And you say the water's slow to come on, Artemis? I nearly burned my hand."

"It's just making a p-point."

Her mother tossed the dirty rag into a bucket and wiped her forehead with the back of her hand. "Artemis. There is something not quite right about a person who treats water as if it were capable of carrying on a conversation."

"If you'd just listen—"

Her mother put her finger to her lips. "Shhh! Keep those thoughts to yourself before they get you—us—into trouble." She rubbed a smudge from the mirror with her sleeve.

"Finish up and meet me in the Calla Lily room. The guests are complaining about ants." On her way out, her mother shook the wrinkles from the bottom of a curtain. "And stay away from that Moonchaser lady," she called. "She's filled your mind with fabrications."

Artemis mopped every tiled corner, then swabbed around the base of the toilet, sink, and tub, hoping she wasn't mopping up any ghostly remnants by mistake. She dumped the water and plopped the mop back into the bucket. Technically her work shift was over. And she knew what would happen in Calla Lily. Poison. Killing. She'd have nothing to do with that. After all, ants were communities of living things. They lived in colonies, and they each had responsibilities just as humans did.

Besides, she had some work of her own to do.

Art's fifth-grade class had studied ecologists, and she'd written a report on Wangari Maathai. She learned about The Green Belt Movement and read Maathai's autobiography, *Unbowed*. She was certain the ghost in the tub was Maathai. But what was she doing hanging out at the hotel? In a tub, no less.

Artemis searched the hotel library for books by Maathai, hoping to find some clues. All she could turn up were two picture books about her which she read curled up on the couch. Just like the adult books she'd used for her research, the picture books described how in Africa, Maathai led groups of impoverished women in planting trees that improved the land and they made a place for themselves in a society that favored men. Teamwork was needed to solve problems.

Art closed the books and looked up at the ceiling. "Ms. Maathai, I thank you for your visit. You'll be a perfect member of my team. I'm going to call us The Sound Seekers Brigade."

7

Warren brought out the best in her. His easygoing nature helped Artemis stay calm, and in order to write a letter to the editor that'd be successful in persuading people just like Wangari Maathai did, Art had to keep her anger in check. She needed to think deeply about what to say and how to say it. Although her salt marsh friends were fantastic, she was lonely for her human one—Warren. She hoped that she could persuade him to join The Sound Seekers Brigade at dinner that night.

But first things first. Dinner for Mom.

Cooking was blissfully straightforward. Everything measured out according to a specific recipe. That night she was preparing "The Best Clam Chowder in New England," one of the most popular items on the Horizons Restaurant's menu. She knew the recipe well, thanks to spending many rainy days in the hotel kitchen with Chef Paul. He demonstrated and Artemis practiced. No talk. Just eyes and hands and taste buds, and the sounds and smells of preparing delicious food. She admired the way Chef Paul moved from cutting board to stove to refrigerator with the focus and ease of a dancer, and she absorbed every little detail as she tagged behind in his wake. When Art cooked with Chef Paul it felt as if her life outside the kitchen belonged to someone else.

She cleaned and chopped the celery and added it to the pot with the onions sizzling in butter. Art flipped on the old radio that used to be her grandmother's. The sound quality was much better than listening to music on her phone.

"Get out those umbrellas, folks, because we're in for a doozy tonight! If you're planning a picnic supper at the beach, better make it early because by six or seven this evening, it'll be a wash-out." Art didn't love traipsing around in wet weather, but the gardens would definitely rejoice.

She poured a bowl of chopped clams and their juices into the soup pot with some milk and let it simmer as she changed into jeans and a fresh T-shirt.

Art scribbled a note on a napkin reminding her mother that she'd been invited to Warren's for dinner. She turned off the stove and grabbed her windbreaker, then set out on her way. As she walked, Art crossed her fingers, wishing Warren's father were working late. She knew she was too old for superstitions, but every so often one crept up on her like a sly old alley cat.

The wind nudged her along, and the sharp, salty smell that tinged the edge of every summer storm tickled her nose. Artemis took a shortcut through the salt marsh toward the woods to check on things.

"RT?" she called, not really expecting him to hear her above the wind. "RT, there's a storm brewing, and I hope you're hunkered down." Art squinted beyond the trail and into the trees beyond it, but everything shook and blurred in the brewing storm. Of course, RT had survived many storms, but who knew what shape he and his family were in after the boys and the BB guns.

Artemis cut away from the trail toward Cove Road, followed it about a quarter of a mile, then took a right on Inlet Avenue and followed that along the shoreline till she came to Warren's house five minutes later. It was a typical beach cottage not unlike the old Muiriel guest house. Warren and his parents were townies like her family; they lived there year-round. Horizon's population almost doubled in size when the summer people arrived, but that wasn't saying much since during the other nine months the population was only a little over three thousand.

Art tapped the door knocker, a white metal seagull with its wings spread wide. Two soft taps plus one loud one for luck. "Hey. Come on in." Warren held his hand out for her windbreaker.

"Hi. I just want to start off by saying that I'll try harder to be more fun."

Warren smiled and hung her windbreaker on a hook by the door. He led her to the deck where his mother sat on a glider, looking through a magazine of knitting patterns.

"Artemis! So glad you could come." Mrs. Lowe looked young, but she was actually Art's mother's age. Her mom had been in the same high school class as Mr. and Mrs. Lowe. Mr. Lowe didn't like her mother much because she had dumped him to go out with Art's father. The fact that her parents were getting a divorce made Mr. Lowe even more spiteful. Warren said his father thought it was wrong for a woman to divorce her husband.

Mrs. Lowe fanned herself with the magazine. "I hear this is the hotel's busiest summer yet. Besides the regular tourists, they're now hosting weddings? Your poor mother must be exhausted."

Not too exhausted to have a boyfriend. "She likes to stay busy."

"Good to hear." Mrs. Lowe rocked back and forth on the glider. "And how is your father's book coming along? A research trip to Greece? How fascinating!"

"Yes. He's loving it, I think." Art counted the spots where the deck paint had bubbled and cracked.

Mrs. Lowe paused, then picked up her magazine. "Well, you two go along. Let me know if you need a hand with dinner." She put her glasses back on and returned to her reading.

In the kitchen Warren offered Art a can of orange soda. She popped the tab off and sipped. Looking around the kitchen, Art whispered, "Where's your d-dad?"

"Not home from work yet." He slugged some soda and

wiped his mouth with the back of his hand. "Wanna help me slice potatoes? I bet I can slice mine more perfect than you."

Warren seemed like he was in a good mood. This was her chance.

"Tell you what. I'll take you up on that challenge if you'll help me with a letter I'm writing to the newspaper editor."

He put his soda aside and started to peel the potatoes. "My spelling's no good."

"No problem. I just need someone to read it to be sure it makes sense."

"About the BBs in the salt marsh?"

She nodded. "People need to notice the salt marsh more. Maybe then they'd care."

"I don't think so," he said.

"Please?" She grabbed a potato and peeler.

"It's too risky."

"So is frying potatoes."

Warren rolled his eyes and put down his peeler. "My name can't be on it."

Because Mr. Lowe would have no problem with boys shooting BBs at birds.

"I'm sending it anonymously," she said.

"Okay. Just this once." Warren put the bowl of potatoes in front of her. "Game on."

Art grinned. "*Chopped Junior*, here I come!" They used to watch that show every Wednesday after school and fantasized about meeting the host, Ted Allen.

Each took a potato and began to slice, working to make every piece the exact same thickness as the one before it.

"I'm right at home with potatoes. Had to chop a ton of them when I made Chef Paul's clam chowder for my mom tonight."

"She's lucky. Havin' a daughter who can cook and all," Warren said.

Art could feel his eyes on her, but she kept hers fixed on

her cutting board. Flushed, she took another potato, sliced it neatly, and held up two slices side by side. "Mine are winners."

"Well, don't be too hasty." He held up two of his own and smiled. "I'm not done yet."

The knives made comfortable, rhythmic swipes on the boards.

"I've never deep-fried anything before," Artemis said.

Warren collected her sliced potatoes and dropped them in a bowl of cold water so they wouldn't turn brown. "Sometimes the grease spatters, but it's no big deal. I've done it a buncha times. No injuries."

A door slammed, and Mr. Lowe lumbered into the room. "Hello, son." He dropped his briefcase on the chair and opened the fridge. "No beer? Again?" The fridge door thunked shut.

Warren glanced at Artemis, then at his father. "Art and I are cooking dinner tonight, Dad."

Mr. Lowe extended his hand to Artemis. "How's the old hotel treating you these days?"

Art kept her eyes down, watching her knife slice potatoes. "F-fine, sir." Out of the corner of her eye, she saw his hand drop.

Mr. Lowe chuckled. "J-j-just fine? N-n-not grrrreat?"

Warren gulped. "Dad, Mom's on the porch. I bet she knows where the beer is."

"Use your head, boy. If there's any beer it'd be right in this here refrigerator, you follow me?"

"Well, I think there's some wine—"

Mr. Lowe's cheeks puffed redder and redder, bulging on the brink of eruption. "Son, you know I don't drink wine." He yanked his pants up by the belt loops. "But I will go to the porch and investigate this oversight with your mother. A man's entitled to his b-beer after a long d-day at work, now ain't that right, M-Miss Artemis?"

Raindrops drummed on the roof and streamed down the windowpane. Art slammed her knife down on the cutting board. Warren winced.

Mr. Lowe put his hands on his hips. "Well, now. Will ya look at that. Your little friend's got a bit o' pepper in her today, don't she, son?" Warren's father shook his head, kicked off his shoes, and left the kitchen. Art glared at his abandoned slip-ons in the middle of the floor.

Warren picked up his father's shoes and put them at the bottom of the staircase. "You know him. He's just a lotta hot air."

"Hot air b-burns," Art said, rinsing off the cutting board and rubbing it dry with a towel, while Warren gathered the potato peels and tossed them into the composter. "He's scary, War. I'm not s-staying this t-time."

"I give him ten minutes before he heads to the hotel bar for beer."

"When he goes, it'd be a good time to talk to your mother about him. I'll come with you if you want."

"Nah, I'm good. Things will be okay." Warren poured oil into a deep skillet and turned on the stove. "Let's start cooking. My fish 'n' chips are awesome."

Artemis pointed at the blue flame curling around the edge of the pan. "You might want to reduce that heat." Warren nodded and guzzled the rest of his soda.

"How do you rate the crispness factor on the fries, Mom?"

Mrs. Lowe squirted a puddle of catsup on her plate. "Ten out of ten this time. Not too greasy either."

Warren high-fived Artemis, then stood and began stacking plates. Art got up to help him. Dinner had been delicious. And calm. Just the three of them.

"If you load the dishes, I'll do the pans when I get back." Mrs. Lowe nibbled another fry.

Warren froze. "Back?"

Thunder rumbled, and Art shivered.

"I've got to make a quick run to the grocery store," she said.

"Mom, wait till the rain stops so you can see where you're going."

"It's not far, honey. No worries."

"Beer isn't that important," he said.

Mrs. Lowe brushed away a few crumbs from her place mat. "I need mayo and bread as well."

Warren sighed. Art juggled a glass on top of a dinner plate, gathered the dirty napkins, and headed to the kitchen. There, Warren rinsed the dishes and handed them to Art to feed into the dishwasher.

"Don't even say it," he said.

Art bit her lip.

He dried his hands and tossed her the towel. "Not worth arguing about, Art, I'm telling you."

The words spewed without warning, sharp and cold. "He shouldn't get away with b-being mean," Art sputtered, loading the last plate into the washer. "Or hurting you. He's an adult. He sh-should know there are b-better ways for people to get what they want."

Warren looked her in the eyes. "Yes. That's something *everyone* should know."

Subtext: I should be nicer.

When Art's anger got the best of her lately, she lashed out. At anybody. But where was the Warren who pinky-promised with her about standing up for each other no matter what? Art felt fire in her chest but persuaded herself to let it burn out. She wasn't about to show that she was in any way like his father.

"What's that line Mr. Baron always says? You can catch more bees—"

"With honey. I know," she said. Their math teacher always recited that phrase when they whined for extra time on a test.

Warren held Art's windbreaker out to her. "Not sure that some people even know what honey is."

"Some people know what it is, they just don't know how to use it," Art replied, slipping her windbreaker on as she followed Warren to the door. "Hey, War?"

"What?" he asked.

"We're still good, right?" She held her breath, hoping it was just his father and not herself that was upsetting him.

"Yup. We're good."

"You'll help me with the letter then?"

"Yup."

"Will you meet me in the hotel library tomorrow morning, around eight? We can knock the letter out in less than a half hour, and then we'll ride our bikes down to the point at Sandpiper Park. That'll check off our third trail for the Summer Cycle Challenge."

Warren's eyes finally twinkled with interest. "Okay, sounds good."

The rain was blinding when Art descended the porch steps of Warren's house. She pulled up her hood and clutched it under her chin. If she had to bargain to get The Sound Seekers Brigade in place, she would.

"Should I walk you home?" Warren called.

Artemis stepped out into the dusk. "Nope. I'm fine," she called over her shoulder. But the wind snatched her words away, somersaulting them through the air like autumn leaves. Sometimes alone was easier.

8

When Artemis reached Cove Road, she attempted to cut back to the salt marsh to check on things. Tree branches swatted her from all sides. Trudging through the brush was nearly impossible, and before long the mucky ground sucked her feet so deep that she lost her sandal and tripped. Once she dug it back out, she removed her other sandal and continued barefoot.

"RT!" she called, scanning the area all around her as the wind-driven rain pelted her face. Bushes that once stood tall slumped over into blurry shadows. She'd never make it to the salt marsh trail at this rate.

"RT, I'll be back tomorrow!" Art tramped back to the road and then took off in a run, bare feet slapping the wet pavement with each stride. She gave up on her hood and soon her loose, wet braid smacked her back. It wouldn't have surprised her to see any number of bizarre things flying through the air—houses, monkeys, witches on bicycles. But Horizons, Connecticut, was no Kansas.

Rounding the corner toward the hotel, she leaped to the left to avoid colliding with a monster branch blocking the driveway. "Agnes! You've lost your limb," she called up to her old elm friend.

Art tugged at the branch and was able to move it a bit but not enough to get it to the side of the road. She figured it had to be two times the length of Chef Paul, about twelve feet long, meaning she shouldn't have been able to budge it at all. Upon closer examination, she found it to be hollow.

Art wiped rain from her eyes and maneuvered around the branch, picking her way past puddles. The tree moaned low and deep and wrapped her branches around herself as if she'd caught a chill.

Art ran her hand along Agnes's rough bark. A chipmunk poked its head from a hollow at the base of the tree and then retreated as quickly as he'd appeared. A squirrel scampered up the trunk and took refuge in a hole about halfway up. Above that, a barn owl perched in the crook of a branch, sheltered by leaves as he stood sentry. Agnes housed them all. "I'm on this, Agnes, don't you worry. I'll find a way to get your strength back."

Art patted Agnes's trunk, then stepped high over the fallen twigs and branches and headed home.

The bright hotel lights guided Artemis through the gray night toward the path to the hotel entrance. Inside the foyer, she shook herself off like she'd seen Prisbrey do after a swim in the Sound, then headed up to the apartment.

"Look at you! I've been worried sick." Her mother put her arm around Art, pulling her inside. "I'm going to heat up some of that wonderful clam chowder you made. That'll warm you right up."

"No thanks, Mom. I ate at Warren's, remember?"

Her mother smoothed down the front of her blouse. "Why didn't his mother or father give you a ride home? It's treacherous out there."

Art dried her hair with a dish towel, thinking there was no way in the world she'd get in a car with Mr. Lowe. "Mom, we need to call the town about Agnes."

"Who?" She ladled chowder into a saucepan and put it on the stove.

"The tree. She's sick and needs an arborist."

Her mother turned the gas burner on, and it lit up with a whoosh. Stirring the chowder, she said, "Honey, you've named a tree?"

"The one at the bottom of the hotel driveway," Art replied.

"Oh. Yes. I know the one. Too late for an arborist. The town's taking that one down. Those weak limbs are an accident waiting to happen."

"But there are t-tons of animals living in it."

"Oh, for goodness' sake. They're wild creatures. They know what to do. They're built for surviving these sorts of things." Her mother stirred the bubbling soup. "Quit making a mountain out of a molehill and have a little soup."

Artemis threw the towel on the floor and kicked it. "I d-do not need soup!"

Her mom tossed the ladle into the sink. "You know what you need? More time indoors," she sputtered. "The outdoors seems to stir you into hissy fits these days. Spend the next few days in the library. The books need to be organized again."

Art picked up the towel and twisted it into a wet knot. "Like that'll m-make everything all better." She snapped the towel against the table leg.

Her mother pointed to Art's bedroom. "Go."

"Fine. I'll t-take care of Agnes myself."

Artemis clomped down the hall. Creatures built for survival? Art wondered if she was sturdy enough to withstand the storm of her very own mother.

Lying on her bed, she rested her eyes on the embroidered pillow her grandmother made when she was born, propped up against the headboard. The nursery rhyme "Rock-a-bye Baby" was stitched on one side, and a cradle hanging from a tree limb was on the other. Sometimes Artemis wished she were little again, back in the days when her mother would hold her and listen and try harder to understand. And then she'd sing that song to her until she fell sleep. Those were the easy days. Growing up was much harder.

9

The next morning, Art woke to the sun playing with her bottle collection. It splashed a prismatic wash on the wall that shifted with each passing minute, just like the changes in the salt marsh. She needed to work fast to keep up. Or work so fast that changes didn't have a chance to happen at all.

She raced downstairs to the kitchen, where Chef Paul and Jess were cracking eggs into a huge bowl. "Chef Paul? Would you mind if I stole some of your compost?"

"Now there's a unique request. I've got enough blueberry cobbler to feed the entire town. Might settle better in your stomach." He gathered up broken eggshells from the counter and dropped them into a compost bin.

"Thanks, but I need to help a sick tree. Fertilizer might do the trick."

"Hmmm," he said. "Depends on the problem. An arborist is the person to ask, but a little compost won't harm in the meantime. Use the stuff from the bin outside the kitchen door. It's been sitting for a few months. I just turned it a week ago and it's looking good."

"There's even seaweed in it this time," Jess said. "I collected it myself."

"Nice! Thanks, you two." Artemis grabbed a box from the recycling closet and a ladle from the utensil wall. "I'll bring this right back, and I'll wash it first, I promise."

After filling the box with compost, Artemis went to Agnes and searched her branches and trunk for any new signs of distress. Luckily, nothing. But no owl or squirrel or chipmunk either. The hollow branch had already been removed.

She used the ladle and her bare hands to dig a trench about

ten inches deep around Agnes's base. "Here you go, Agnes," she said. "Let's do Wangari Maathai proud." She ladled the compost into it, then covered it over with dirt so it wouldn't attract pests. "Lots of good stuff in here, straight from Chef Paul's five-star kitchen. Oh—and from the ocean too. You'll be feeling better in no time."

Artemis dashed back inside and made it upstairs to fix breakfast before her mom emerged from her bedroom. She poured coffee beans into the grinder and despite doing it daily, the screech stung her ears. She liked the smell of coffee but not the taste. Nothing was entirely black or white, it seemed. Not coffee. Not nature. Not people or ghosts.

After breakfast, Artemis went to the hotel library to accomplish her next task. Besides zillions of books, this library contained interesting, and possibly valuable, antiques. She loved the old space, but her mom claimed it was an eyesore. Thankfully, Mr. Hellander hadn't remodeled the library. It was considered a low traffic room, way down on his to-do list. He had run out of money before he could get to it.

Art sat at the desk, leaning over to inhale the worn, leather-topped surface that smelled earthy, like moss in the woods. Black ink spots and scratches marred the surface. Had someone in the Muiriel family been a writer or a teacher? Perhaps Mr. Hellander's uncle?

"Art?" Warren slid through the door and into the library.

"Yes! Thanks for coming, Warren. Pull up a chair." Warren grabbed a folding chair from the corner of the room and set it up at the desk beside Artemis. "So, here's the deal," she said. "I need to write a persuasive letter. I want to make people care about Long Island Sound and the salt marsh. Maybe they'll even join my team."

"Team?"

"Actually, we'll be more than a team. We'll be a strong bunch of allies ready to defend Long Island Sound and its

shores. We're called The Sound Seekers Brigade. Has a nice
ring to it, don't you think?"

"Okay, so you need to be specific about what your team—
er, brigade—needs to do. It could be like when Mrs. Alibee
was recruiting more kids for the school play. She ran it like
a job ad."

"Right! 'Wanted: A few good kids to light up the stage
with star power!' or something like that. Great idea." Art
jotted down a few things in her field notebook and handed it
to Warren. "What do you think?"

Warren read it. "Mrs. Alibee made it sound like joining
the theater club was like a prize. Can't you make this sound a
bit more…well, worthwhile?" Artemis wrote some more and
slid the notebook to Warren. He read and nodded. "Much
better. I'll read it aloud like Ms. Smythe tells us to do after
we write something. Best way to get the bugs out." He stood
and cleared his throat.

"Dear Editor,

Wanted: A few concerned citizens to join The Sound
Seekers Brigade. Why? Because Long Island Sound and
its salt marshes are under attack.

I've lived in Horizons for years and have always enjoyed
visiting the beach and nature trails. Lately, I've been
shocked to see trash building up in the salt marsh grasses.
It strangles plants and puts birds in danger. Our community counts on the beach area not just for our own fun,
but because it brings income from tourists. We count on
the salt marsh to stay healthy and intact so the Sound
doesn't flood our properties.

There's a war going on, and we need members who will
speak up when they see people riding bikes in nature pre-
serves or disturbing nests with BB guns or disrespecting
plants and animals in other ways. We need to form a
brigade that will work together to defend our precious

Long Island Sound and its salt marshes. Please join The Sound Seekers Brigade. Help us keep our Sound sound.

Thank you,
A Concerned Citizen"

Artemis grinned. "Perfect. I can't email it to the newspaper if we want to stay anonymous, so I'll write it over neatly, and we can drop it off on our way to Sandpiper Park."

A knock interrupted them, and Artemis tiptoed to the door. The doorknob jiggled, and they heard footsteps retreating down the hall. Art cracked open the door and peeked outside. She shrugged. "Probably just some kid playing around," Art said, locking the door.

She turned to a blank page in her notebook and began to write the letter in her best penmanship.

Another knock sounded, but it didn't come from the library door. Warren jabbed his finger toward the bookcase of classics, and Art went over to investigate. Everything appeared to be in its place. Just shelves of old books with broken spines. All the books were organized by genre and alphabetized according to the author's last name. Art and her mother had spent two days arranging them last summer, so she knew the system.

Again came the sound of knocking.

Artemis jumped back, her heartbeat thrumming in her ears. Something was behind that wall, behind the collection of books by Charles Dickens.

"What's going on?" Warren asked, wringing his hands.

"It could be Simon Rodia, and I'm dying to meet him," Art whispered in an attempt to persuade herself to be brave.

"What're you talkin' about?" Warren whispered back.

"Never mind. I'll fill you in later. Help me move these books."

Art removed an armload of books and laid them on the floor.

"Look!" Warren exclaimed, pointing at a vertical crack that appeared between the shelves. They emptied more shelves until a small door was revealed. Art ran her fingers along the edge, feeling for a knob. Finding nothing, she gave the door a tiny push. It opened just enough for her to peek in, but it was so dark she couldn't tell what was what. Her knees wobbled and her arms goose-bumped, but Art reminded herself that Simon Rodia had climbed great heights—literally—to build the Watts Towers, and Wangari Maathai went to jail for speaking up. She would follow their brave lead.

Artemis jostled and tugged at the three bottom shelves, finally removing each one. "Wait for me here, War."

"What? Why go in there?" he asked.

"I need to do it for The Sound Seekers Brigade. You'll see."

There was just enough space for her to duck down and wiggle through the door. Inside she flicked on her phone flashlight, revealing a narrow hallway that rose to a ceiling a foot or so above her head. Art moved the bright beam along the walls. "There's a door at the end of this hallway, War." Artemis moved toward it with tiny steps, her stomach flip-flopping.

"Come back, Artemis!" he said. "You don't know what's in there."

Art reached for the doorknob and then pulled back her hand.

"Mr. Rodia?" she asked, giving the door a quick knock. "Are you there?"

Turning the knob, she pushed against the door, but it wouldn't budge. She turned it the other way and pulled. No luck. She reached up, feeling above the door to see if a key had been left on the ledge, but all she discovered was dust.

"Rats. I've gotten this far, and now I can't go on," she muttered.

"Oh, I think you can," a voice taunted. Artemis spun around and searched the hallway with her phone light.

"Warren, was that you?" she called, trying to keep her voice from trembling.

"No!" Warren yelled. "Just get back here."

Art looked at the ceiling. "Mr. Rodia?"

"Deedee," the voice said. It was a faint, low voice, so thin that a slight breeze might carry it away.

Artemis's phone light fell upon an item she'd missed earlier—a black top hat hung on a nail midway up one wall. She reached for it without thinking and placed it on her head. It covered her ears and she could barely see from under the wide brim. She pushed it further back on her head and it fell to the floor. The strange, low voice giggled.

"It's n-not funny," Art protested as she tried to replace the hat on the nail. But it kept falling off.

The voice chuckled again, clearly amused at her fumbling.

"Be quiet!" Art snapped.

"Sometimes quiet is a good idea. Sometimes not," the voice said. "Sometimes silence—"

Art could barely make out the words as they seemed to circle around her and then slide underneath the locked door. And then—coincidentally?—there was silence.

"W-wait! Finish the sentence," she said as she jiggled the doorknob harder and harder. Art stepped back from the locked door. "Sometimes silence stinks, that's what. It'd be p-polite if you'd answer me at least." She held her breath waiting for a response.

Silence.

"Great. Have it your w-way." She hung the hat easily on the nail. Was she trembling less? "Some questions never get answered," she said as she stomped back down the hall toward the library.

She pulled the secret door closed behind her, and Warren grabbed her arm. "What went on in there, Artemis?" he asked.

Artemis looked him in the eye. "Did you hear a strange voice?"

"No! I only heard you."

"Okay…then it was a ghost."

"Oh, c'mon, Art, really? First, you're talkin' to plants and whatnot, and now you're talkin' to ghosts?"

"Possibly. I think so. I guess." She shrugged. "I can't scientifically prove it, but my gut says there are ghosts around this hotel. Nice ones, so don't worry about it."

She slid the shelves back into place and put back the books they'd removed. Warren just stared at her, eyes wide, mouth agape.

"I'm sure the ghosts are here for a reason, and it's not to hurt us," she said.

"I—I don't believe in ghosts," Warren whispered, his face drained of color.

"Fine. It's not like anyone's forcing you to go into that hidden hallway. But I'm going to figure out what's going on around here, and if it means going back in there, I will."

Artemis was a master at recognizing patterns, and the ghosts' behaviors appeared to be settling into one, teasing her by appearing and disappearing when she called for Simon Rodia. Maybe this Deedee ghost was in the library because he too had written a book. And like Maathai and Rodia, maybe he'd be a valuable addition to The Sound Seekers Brigade.

She jumped up and scoured the nonfiction section of the library.

"Wait. I thought we were done here," Warren implored. "We wrote the letter, so what about the bike ride?"

"If I don't find anything in fifteen minutes, I'll quit searching."

Warren sighed and flopped down into an overstuffed orange chair. "Find what?"

"You'll see."

Warren stood. "You know, I'll just go get my bike and wait for you by the shed. But if you're not out in fifteen, I'm going by myself."

"Okay," she said, running her finger along the shelf.

Artemis found the authors whose last names began with D. Not many, and no match for Deedee. Maybe Deedee actually stood for initials, like D.D., and wasn't his surname. She looked again, more carefully. "Ta-da!" She pulled out a paperback book about a man named Jay Norward "Ding" Darling, published by the Ding Darling Wildlife Society.

Ding Darling received the Pulitzer Prize—twice—for editorial cartooning. One cartoon titled "The Charge of the Nature Lovers Brigade" shows a group of picnickers arriving at a beautiful outdoor spot, but when they leave, there are holes in the ground where the bushes were, and trees picked clean of leaves. Another cartoon shows a hunter shooting ducks; years later, there are tons of hunters but no ducks at all. Clearly, Darling didn't find hunting or disturbing nature funny. He just used cartoons to catch your eye and make you look.

Flipping through the rest of the book, Art spotted a man wearing a black wide-brimmed hat in some of the pictures, exactly like the hat she'd seen in the hallway.

"Awesomazing!" It had to have been Ding Darling laughing at her back there. She decided to forgive him. Judging from what she read, he wasn't the cruel type. Maybe a bit playful, but not cruel.

She slid the book into her pack, put away her phone, and exited the library, pulling the door closed behind her.

"Artemis, what are you doing in the library with the door locked?" Mr. Hellander demanded. "I came by earlier and couldn't get in. I was just getting ready to call maintenance."

Art struggled to thread her shaky arms through the backpack straps. "N-nothing. It must have locked b-by mistake."

"Doors don't lock by mistake." Mr. Hellander opened the door. "This is a public room open to all guests." He entered and walked around, scowling, looking in corners and under tables. "What are you hiding in here?"

"Nothing. My mother t-told me to straighten it up."

Then Art saw something that stopped her heart—the secret door! In her hurry to reshelve the books, she'd misplaced some of them, and the gap exposed the secret door, slightly ajar. She was sure she'd closed it firmly behind her.

"D-did you hear that, Mr. Hellander?" Art asked, in a desperate attempt to divert his attention from the bookshelf. "R-rita! I hear Rita at the front desk calling you." Sometimes a little white lie was necessary.

Mr. Hellander looked at his watch. "It's too early for my nine a.m. appointment to be here. Rita can wait." He wagged his index finger at Artemis. "I've a good mind to talk to your mother about your behavior lately."

She gulped and focused on some cigarette burns in the rust-colored Oriental rug.

"I'm sure she wouldn't approve of you sneaking around doing who-knows-what behind locked doors. Artemis Sparke, your head is always in the clouds. You need to take up some normal kid activities this summer. Frisbee. Or sailing. Back in the day, I even won a regatta or two." Then, after another stern look in her direction, he left, striding off toward the front desk.

Artemis quickly closed the secret door, then went outside to the shed, but Warren was gone.

Back upstairs, lying on her bed, her muscles melted into the mattress, limp as overcooked linguine. She flipped to the middle of her field notebook and turned down the corner of the page. She labeled this section Ecologist Ghosts. It made sense to collect as much information as she could about these people and record it, just as she did with her salt marsh observations. After all, each ghost left mysterious clues, just like RT and the others in the salt marsh. She just needed to pay close attention.

Art leafed through Ding Darling's book, then took out her colored pencils. He excelled in subtlety, using cartoons to get people to take nature seriously. Mrs. Moonchaser might even call it subtext. She copied a few of Darling's cartoons, then tried some of her own. Not so difficult. She felt a plan coming on, a plan that didn't scream anger. She would try humor.

10

Over there, Jess. That tree is a perfect spot." Artemis pointed her flashlight at mid-trunk. The night air rustled the stack of posters under her arm, and she handed one to Jess, along with a few thumbtacks.

"This one's great, Art! Where'd you learn to draw like this?"

"Didn't. It just came to me after looking at a few cartoons by other artists. You believe in ghosts, Jess?"

"My dad does, so let's just say I'm open to the idea."

"Good to know. Because rumor has it that this hotel has a few. Nice ones, that is." Jess's forehead crinkled, and she glanced warily over her shoulder. "Don't worry, I'll explain later. So, you think these posters will make people pay more attention to the salt marsh?"

"I don't know how they could avoid it. Gosh, that sea monster looks like something out of a horror movie." Jess put in the last tack and pulled out her phone. "I need a picture of this."

"It's not supposed to be attractive. It's supposed to make a point."

"Mission accomplished," Jess said.

The two girls continued hanging Art's posters around the neighborhood, ducking into the bushes whenever a car came around the bend. After the tenth one was tacked to a streetlamp pole, they shut off the flashlight and headed back to the hotel.

"Thanks for helping, Jess. I owe you one."

"No problem. I hope they help."

Art put her hand on Jess's shoulder. "And for your dedicated service, I hereby make you an official member of The Sound Seekers Brigade."

"What does that mean?"

"Just what it says. We seek ways to keep Long Island Sound sound. You know, healthy."

Jess saluted. "At your service."

As they approached the hotel entrance, Artemis shielded her eyes from the numerous lights along the walkway. "Jeez. No wonder I haven't seen any fireflies lately. Can't expect them to hang around when it's so bright."

"Come to think of it, I haven't seen many this summer either," Jess said.

"They'll avoid the area if they can't send their light codes out to attract a mate. No mate, no babies. Then no fireflies at all."

Art crouched down to examine the underside of a light. "Just a simple bulb here," she murmured. With a flick of her wrist, she unscrewed the bulb, then proceeded to remove all the others.

"Art, what are you doing?" Jess said, holding her hand over her mouth and looking all around. "If anyone sees you, you're dead."

"With the lights on, the fireflies are as good as dead."

Jess scurried ahead and went into the hotel. Artemis looked over her shoulder at the dark walkway. She smiled to herself, put the bulbs in her backpack, and followed her friend.

In the hotel lobby, three women sat around a table playing cards while a fourth read to them from the *Horizons Sentinel*.

"Well, I'll be," she said when she finished reading. "Pretty dramatic letter to the editor, using the term *war* to describe a little pollution."

"Nettie, be real!" another one said. "The writer's speaking

figuratively to show how serious the matter is." She slapped a card down and drew another from the deck.

"I'm on vacation. I don't want to think about war, ladies." The third woman placed her cards on the table. "Gin! Sheila, it's your deal."

Art walked back toward the kitchen, not quite sure if she should feel happy or sad.

11

The next day, Artemis found Warren at the beach, scrubbing the outside of his rowboat with a stiff brush. "Hey, Warren. Did you see our letter in the paper?" she asked.

He stopped scrubbing. The barnacles on the blue boat looked like barley stuck on the bottom of Chef Paul's soup pot. "My father saw it," he said.

She gulped. "He d-doesn't—"

"He doesn't know it was us. But still."

"What did he say?"

"Said if people felt so strongly about somethin' that they'd write a letter about it, then they shouldn't be afraid to sign their name." He continued to scrub. "He said the letter was weak. A lotta fluff. He said that boys will be boys."

The fact that Warren's dad thought all boys liked shooting birds with BBs made her eyes burn. "I overheard a b-bunch of ladies in the lobby talking about the letter. Yeah, they didn't all agree on what was important, but at least our letter got them thinking."

Art shifted her bare feet, digging in to get to the cooler, damp sand beneath the surface. She bent over and made eye contact with Warren. "Hello?"

"I hear ya."

"Jess and I put up some posters around the neighborhood last night."

"Not about boys with BB guns, I hope."

"No. Animals, plants, and stuff. They're funny. Keep your eye out and let me know if you see people reading them. I'm dying to know what people think."

Warren kept scrubbing, so hard that paint started to peel off with the barnacles. Art saw a boy and his father over by the dock, struggling to get a dragon-shaped kite airborne before it took a hard hit on the beach. "Warren, I hate that your dad has this p-power over you."

"Yeah, well, I gotta live with the guy."

"I know. I just wish I could help."

"I'll let you know when you can. Meanwhile, you know puttin' posters up on private property is trespassing, right?"

"Julia Butterfly Hill sat in a redwood tree for 738 days. She t-trespassed to make a point against cutting them down. And it worked."

He picked some scales of blue paint from the bristles of his brush. Art put her hand out before he could flick them onto the sand, and he sprinkled them into her palm. She brushed the paint chips into her pocket and took a deep breath of sea air. "I'm sorry your dad doesn't approve of what I'm doing, Warren. But the salt marsh is in horrible shape. Nature is trying to tell me something."

"Artemis, I know you believe in some kinda bird language. But nature doesn't speak in a human voice. Just like I doubt there are voices and ghosts in the secret hallway in the library."

"I d-don't understand everything. But somehow I understand how Mother Nature f-feels."

He began to scrub again. Hard, as though his life depended on it. "Art, it's safer for me to stick to fishin' and boats. My dad thinks environmentalists are crazy. His word, not mine."

The kite fell into the water, and the little boy cried as his father held him tight to prevent him from running into the waves to rescue it.

"Okay then." Art turned to leave. "If you change your mind and want to be a part of The Sound Seekers Brigade, even as a secret member, just let me know."

Warren dropped the brush in the bucket. "You wanna go up and get a couple sodas from Jake?"

"You're changing the s-subject."

"I'm thirsty."

Art kicked at the sand, spraying it in all directions. "Do you even c-care about me anymore?" she yelled. Two fishermen who'd just docked their boat watched her mini-tantrum. Art tried to ignore them by picking barnacles off the boat.

Warren rubbed sand from his eye. "Look, I'm sorry," he said. "Let's just go get a couple sodas, and we can talk about it."

"F-forget it," she snapped, flicking the barnacle at his feet, then kicking at the bow of the boat. Warren's face drooped, and Art immediately regretted her behavior.

"You're not gonna get what you want by kicking and yelling," he said.

"Hey! Hey, you!" One of the fishermen walked toward Artemis. "You're old enough to know better." He pointed at the children down the beach. "What kind of example are you setting for them?"

Art's cheeks flushed. "I—I'm..." *A crazy girl. Just like people say.* She spun around and walked away. *Warren probably wishes he could scrub me away as easily as the barnacles on his boat.*

A scream came from the other end of the beach. Art ran toward it, nearly stepping on a dead fish that'd washed ashore. *Shrieks and Death on the Beach.* It sounded like a bad movie title.

"Mommy! Mommy!" A little girl in a blue sun hat was crying. She had a plastic shovel in one hand and held her other hand out to her mother.

"What happened, Lily?"

Lily dropped the shovel and pointed toward the water. Her mother looked out and her lips curled back in disgust.

She scooped up her daughter and raced toward the hotel.

Artemis darted to where the girl had been digging and scanned the water. A humongous pack of jellyfish floated on the surface just about twelve feet from the shore. A jelly-fish bloom! It made sense; the less fish around to eat them, the more jellies there would be. Plus, with the ocean getting warmer and warmer, jellies would thrive better and longer. The resemblance to one of Art's posters was uncanny. She took a step back from the water, examined the sand at her feet, and stepped even further back onto dry sand. Jellies get tangled in motorboat blades, and their parts disperse over a wide area. People often got stung by stepping on tentacles on the beach.

Art's stomach heaved, and she yelled to the jellyfish, "Stay back! Please, not so close!" The mound of jellyfish moved as one, the center rising and drawing in the edges like a balloon, inflating and deflating as it made its way back out to sea. Art always checked the water in August before jumping off Warren's boat for a swim. By that time of year, the Sound had warmed up enough to lure the jellyfish back, and she wanted to avoid any close encounters. Now that she'd seen this crowd of them—at the end of June, no less—she'd probably give up swimming altogether.

"What's going on out here?" Mr. Hellander ran toward her, kicking up sand with his big leather shoes. His navy necktie, dotted with white dolphins, swung back and forth like a windshield wiper. He shielded his eyes and looked out at the water. "What happened to Lily Ellington?"

"Not sure. She was digging in the sand and all of a s-sud-den she s-started to yell." Art pointed to the retreating fleet of jellyfish.

Mr. Hellander squinted. "What?"

She pointed again. "Jellyfish. They're probably m-man o' wars. Big stingers."

"What jellyfish?" He scanned the area.

She pointed again. "R-right there."

"Lily and her mother didn't say anything about jellyfish. And I don't see a thing." He walked along the shore, apparently looking for some clue as to what might have alarmed Lily.

Art sat on the dock and recorded the facts in her field notebook. It had been impossible to count individual jellyfish in the bloom, so she sketched the mound of jellies as one, along with the dock and beach and the two Sailfishes anchored offshore. She drew everything to scale to emphasize the size of the jellyfish bloom.

Mr. Hellander trudged over. "Keep your supposed sightings to yourself, Artemis." The front of his shirt was drenched with sweat, and he loosened his tie. "No sense in upsetting people over a hallucination." Art continued to sketch. "And I don't think I'm hallucinating when I continue to see you over at our trouble-making neighbor's house," he said.

"She's the s-smartest woman I know."

"You two have your heads in the clouds. You're full of nothing but fluff. Better to channel your imagination into drawing pictures."

Art snapped her field notebook closed and shrugged her backpack over her shoulders, hoping Mr. Hellander hadn't seen enough to make any connections between her sketch and the poster they'd tacked to the tree trunk.

"Sometimes t-truth is way worse than what you can imagine," she muttered under her breath.

Mr. Hellander yanked his necktie from his shirt collar and snapped it at the sand like a whip. "You'll keep your thoughts to yourself if you know what's good for you."

Speak up or shut up? Some days it was impossible to know which to do.

12

On her way to check on Agnes, Artemis noticed that the poster she and Jess had tacked to the boathouse was gone. So was the one tacked to the bulletin board at the dock.

"No!" she cried, pulling tacks from the wall. "This war is escalating every day. I've got to up my game."

From a distance, Agnes looked okay. As she got closer, though, Art noticed the soil around her base was sprouting tiny green leaves. When she bent to inspect the seedlings, the odor was obvious—mint.

"How did mint grow from compost? And how could anything grow so fast anyway?" She picked a sprig and nibbled it. "Yup. Definitely mint." She looked up into the tree's crown. "Doesn't seem like it'll hurt you, Agnes. Maybe it'll be a magic cure. You never know."

Art patted Agnes's trunk and went to meet her mother for lunch. As she passed the bar, she overhead snatches of conversation coming from inside.

"Our neighbor…Marion Moonchaser." It was Jake, the bartender. "She's concerned about the hotel. Too much noise. Too many people."

"That's what she gets for living in a tourist town," a deep voice responded.

Dad?

"And with Union City and Narraganset opening new hotels, Harry's feeling even more pressure to keep up," Jake said.

"Before you know it, Horizons will have a boardwalk and vendors. Might be kind of fun."

Art peeked around the corner. Her father wore a denim jacket over a pink polo shirt, khaki shorts, and sandals. His skin was tanned, and it looked as though he'd polished his face with the stuff he used on his car tire rims.

Jake closed the dishwasher. "The town needs tourist business. But we don't want to become another Atlantic City."

"Just keeping up with the times, Jake. Gotta do it." Her dad took a swallow of his drink. "Actually, I take that back. Look at Greece. The Parthenon. All the old stuff preserved. You should've seen it, Jake. More magnificent than any picture in a history book." He wiped his mouth with the back of his hand. "Instead of all her complaining, Mrs. Moonchaser should figure out a way to protect the old while still keeping up with the times."

Why is everyone so mean to Mrs. Moonchaser?

Artemis stepped into the bar. Jake looked up and flagged her down with his dish rag. "Artemis! Look who's home!" He pointed to her father, who gave her a weak wave. "Come on in and have a soda, listen to your dad's stories about Greece."

Art sat on the stool two over from her dad and put her backpack on the seat between them.

Jake poured Art a tall glass of ginger ale. He dropped two cherries into it, along with a dash of cherry juice, the way she used to drink it when she was little. "Here you go, kiddo," he said as he set down a basket of cinnamon rolls. "Courtesy of Chef Paul."

Her dad held his glass up and said, "Cheers, Artemis. Happy summer." He clinked his glass to hers.

Art took a sip of her drink. "Summer's not happy for p-people who get c-criticized for speaking up."

He cleared his throat. "What do you mean?"

"P-People need to quit attacking Mrs. Moonchaser."

"Yes. Well. Anyway, I'm sorry I wasn't around much the last few months. Things got a little difficult with a student or two at school, and most of my free time was devoted to putting out fires and working on my book."

Jake jumped in. "Really, Garrett? You're writing a book? About what, Greek urns and pyramids and stuff?"

"The book doesn't cover Egypt and pyramids," her father said. "It focuses strictly on classical Greek architecture and how it influences our modern buildings."

"We have an author in our midst, Artemis. How about that?" Jake poured tomato juice into two glasses and topped them off with lemon wedges for a couple of women at the other end of the bar.

"Publish or perish. I need to keep my job, Jake." He turned to Artemis. "What have you been up to this summer?"

"N-not much." Art plucked a cherry from her drink and popped it into her mouth.

"Not much?" Jake countered. "Give yourself some credit. How about the hours you spend doing housekeeping? And your daily walks to the salt marsh picking up trash?"

"Artemis! There you are." Her mother hurried into the bar. "Are you finished in the library already?" She stopped short. "Garrett, back from Greece already?"

"Hello, Ellen. Yes, it was wonderful. Beautiful. You should go there one day."

"That would be nice."

"Sit for a minute," he said to her. "I stopped in for a coffee on my way to the university and hoped I'd run into you both. First off, are you going to stay with me on weekends this month, Art? I'd sure like that."

"I c-can't leave the beach. Or the hotel. I have lots t-to do here," she said, taking a cinnamon roll from the basket.

"My house is only a bike ride away, remember?"

"I think we can work that out, right, Artemis?" her mom replied. "Anyway, I could use some time alone."

To hang out with Mr. Hellander. That's what this is about.

"Great," her father said. "And second, I was hoping you'd continue your speech therapy this summer. Just once a week."

"N-no way. Waste of t-time."

"But your teacher said you made great progress this year," her mom countered.

Here we go again, the never-ending argument that I always lose. "K-kids still think I'm weird." She focused on the bubbles rising in her soda to distract herself from the conversation that was bound to leave her miserable.

"But you *can* get better," her father said.

"You know, Artemis," her mother said, putting her hand on Art's shoulder, "your aunt stuttered too."

"But I'm not anything like D-Dad's sister!" she protested, her eyes welling with tears. "I will n-never be a successful lawyer!"

"Of course not. And that's not the point. You're named after her because we loved her like we love you."

Artemis rolled her eyes. Her father rubbed his eyes.

Her mom fished a lipstick out of her purse, and a stack of papers dropped out. She reached down to gather them, but not before Dad grabbed a stack first.

"A Sound Alert? What's this all about?" he asked, flipping through the pages. "What is this? A gigantic jellyfish holding an unsuspecting child on a spoon?" He grinned.

Art bit her lower lip and tasted blood.

Her father picked up another one. "Look at this one! The land's crumbling underneath beach houses as they fall into the ocean. And that house is calling for help before it drowns! Clever."

An indirect compliment, Art thought with quiet pride, but she'd take it.

Her mother snatched the posters from his grasp and stuffed them back into her purse. "Don't mind these. Some prankster is just trying to get a rise out of the tourists."

"Why do you have them?" He leaned in close to her, chuckling. "Are *you* the prankster?"

"Of course not. I removed every one I could find so the hotel guests wouldn't get upset. If Harry—"

He raised his eyebrows. "He's Harry now?"

"I am merely trying to do what's best for the hotel. As an employee, I have a vested interest in its success."

"Very loyal of you." He pointed at the posters. "So, who's behind the cartoons?"

Art shifted slightly in her chair, pretending to be absorbed by the eleven o'clock news blaring on the television behind them.

"Marion Moonchaser is a prime suspect. She's already caused many problems for this hotel."

"Just b-because she wants a little p-peace and quiet does not make her guilty," Art said, glowering.

"She's gone too far. The bulbs in the lanterns along all the walkways were tampered with. Mrs. Anderson fell last night trying to make her way to the terrace."

Art had never considered that her plans might backfire and harm people instead of helping them. She couldn't let Mrs. Moonchaser take the blame.

"Maybe it was just a summer p-prank by a bunch of bored kids."

"Don't be naïve, Artemis. That woman has made it clear that she intends to darken and silence this hotel. What she's done is illegal."

"You n-never liked her."

"If she wants to prove herself innocent, then she needs to respond to Harry's papers."

"P-Papers?"

Her mother unraveled a cinnamon roll. "Cease and desist order. Staying silent just makes her look guilty." She popped a bite into her mouth and wiped her sticky hands.

"She is not g-guilty of anything!"

Her mom pulled out the posters and shook them in Art's face. "Then who do you think did this?"

Artemis's mouth dropped open, but no words came out. A brave girl would confess, she knew. Wangari Maathai hadn't been afraid to speak up. Even if it meant she would go to jail.

"You better not be involved in this, Artemis," her mother said. "Harry said he saw you at her house, and I distinctly told you to stay away." She shoved the posters back into her purse. "So, stay away."

The news anchor droned on about a tropical storm forming in the Gulf. Her mother yanked a cocktail napkin from the holder and smoothed it out on the counter as if it had a thousand wrinkles. She took a pen from her purse. "Okay, Garrett. What's your schedule like these next few weeks? Your daughter could use some attention, and I could use a break."

Artemis closed her eyes and willed her parents to disappear, but when she opened them, they were still there, and the news anchor warned of possible tornados.

13

Art pulled the library door closed with a sigh. Only a few more shelves to organize, and then she'd be free. But it couldn't hurt to take one little peek before starting work. This time, she easily uncovered the entrance, slid through the secret door, and closed it behind her. Using her phone flashlight, she inched down the hallway, passing Ding Darling's hat on the hook. She ran her fingers along the brim, then lifted it off the hook and put it on. She shook her head. The hat didn't move. This time, it felt settled and serene as it rested on her head, the brim just above her eyebrows.

Peering out from under it, she called, "Helloooo? Anybody home?" and beamed her light up and down the hall. "I'm looking for you, Mr. Rodia. I need to ask you a few things." The light landed on the locked door at the end of the hallway, and she headed toward it.

Schwoop! A flimsy figure dropped like a curtain right in front of her. She jumped and choked back a scream. The figure tipped his black tweed newsboy cap to her in a gentlemanly fashion and bowed deeply.

Art blinked fast and tipped her own hat back at him.

He was much shorter than Chef Paul, and his black pants and jacket hung loosely, as if he'd lost a lot of weight. "Are you Simon Rodia?" she asked.

He reached deep into the pocket of his coat and pulled out a handful of something—Scrabble tiles?—and leaned over and sprinkled them on the floor. The tiles sparkled in the beam of her phone light as if they'd just been polished. Art crouched down to get a better look. They looked like broken shards of china or porcelain. A number of pieces were blue and white, others green, and a few were patterned in red and yellow. Their edges felt smooth and soft with age. She looked up, and the ghost's dark eyes crinkled at the edges. He pointed to the shards on the floor.

"I can't d-deal with these broken pieces right now. I have other things I need to put back together. I was h-hoping you'd help since you're good at that. If you're Simon Rodia, that is." The ghost nodded, pointing again at the shards. "In a minute. Right now I need you to join my team, The Sound Seekers Brigade. Can you give me some ideas about how I can get people to pay more attention to the outdoors around them?"

His finger jabbed again at the tiles scattered across the floor.

"Okay, already," Art said with a sigh. "Fine. I'll do for you if you'll do for me."

She picked two shards up and compared them, put them side by side to see if they might fit together or if they looked similar, perhaps pieces from the same object. When she looked back up to ask the ghost a question, he was gone.

Of course he was.

"Quit playing around! What happened to helping each other? Now I'm left with n-nothing."

But the shiny pieces intrigued Artemis. She fiddled with them, and with a little trial and error she finally fit them all together. They formed a kind of collage with the words, *Dream Big*, scrolled in yellow along the bottom. All those shards, those cast-offs, had transformed, under her fingers, into a beautiful mosaic, a mini-mural!

It was one thing to dream big, but making that dream happen was quite another thing, she thought.

Artemis didn't want to disturb the mosaic, but she worried about leaving it on the floor even though, as far as she knew, she was the only one who knew about the secret hallway. She snapped a picture with her phone and, as an extra safety measure, emailed it to herself. That way, she could reassemble the pieces with the help of the photo when she got back to her room.

Outside, dark was descending, and a brisk sea breeze animated the trees, casting shadows on the hallway walls that swooped and plunged like hawks diving for voles. She took off Ding's hat and set it on the ground, then gathered the pottery shards and carefully deposited them into it. She didn't think Ding Darling would mind if she borrowed his hat for a day or two.

On the floor of her bedroom, Artemis reconstructed the mosaic so it looked just like the photo. Using her magnifying glass, she zoomed in on every tiny detail. Some of the tiles were the same color, and groups of them shared a distinctive design. Maybe each group came from a different object. The mosaic was ten pieces wide and five tall. Fifty pieces altogether. Were they from five teacups? Five dinner plates? Five pots?

Art peered closer and noticed that underneath the words *Dream Big*, something else was etched. She struggled to make sense of the faded letters. S_mon Rod_a.

Confirmed. Simon Rodia.

She googled him. Facts: He built the Watts Towers in Los Angeles, seventeen towers decorated with found objects—tiles, broken bottles, seashells, mirrors, and more. He called the towers *Nuestro Pueblo*. It was Spanish for Our Town. He built the towers single-handedly in his neighborhood, one that was quite neglected. But the community rallied around him. The towers brought the people together. He'd beautified a place many people avoided, by transforming trash into public art that people cared about.

Now his advice to "Dream Big" made sense.

Gathering up the tiles, Art returned them to the hat, then shoved the hat way back on her closet shelf.

Artemis recorded all the new information in her field notebook on the special page for ecologist ghosts and sketched the mural right next to her sketch of Ding Darling's hat.

"So, now what? I know Mr. Rodia liked to take what he had and go with it. So, whatever I need to succeed, it's probably right here in front of me. Hidden in plain sight."

14

Within minutes of hiding the mosaic shards, Art was startled by the sound of horns beeping and people screaming. Through the open window she saw a tour bus of people armed with cameras and binoculars, swarming the Horizons Hotel beach. The sand dunes were littered with picnic refuse that buzzed with flies.

Artemis high-tailed it outside.

"Do you see it, Gerry?" a woman yelled at her husband, who scanned the water with binoculars.

"Nope. Not even a regular-size jellyfish."

"Keep looking! I need a picture of that monster to show the grandkids."

No way was this about my posters.

The card-playing women exited the hotel, dragging their suitcases behind them. "I told you there was something odd about this town, Nettie, with all its talk of wars and what-have-you."

"I hear you, my friend. We'll get our money back and finish our vacation elsewhere in a few weeks. Somewhere more peaceful."

The hotel parking lot erupted with agitated drivers trying to park and set foot on the now-famous Jellyfish Beach. Mr. Hellander attempted to direct the traffic, but nobody paid attention to him. One car sideswiped another, and the drivers swore at each other while kids in wet bathing suits, holding drippy ice cream cones, looked on.

All of a sudden, Art's mother was there, running toward the cars, waving her hands, trying to help Mr. Hellander stop the madness. But the noise just got louder, and soon two cop cars arrived. Art ran over to her mom, who was begging the cops to help and didn't even notice Artemis at her side. Unfortunately, Mr. Hellander did.

"Artemis! Get out of here right now. Somehow, I think you're involved in this mess. You and that dastardly neighbor of ours. Now git!" Mr. Hellander shouted.

"I'll—I c-can help—" Her mouth wasn't capable of saying more than a few words to the man, even if they were nice words.

"Just go! My hotel thrives on facts, not fantasies, and you're too full of the latter to be of any help," he yelled.

As she turned to leave, she came face to face with the Barlow twins.

"Chaos! Cool!" Henry said while his brother filmed it all on his phone.

Artemis pushed the phone away. "Quit it! C-can't you be d-decent human beings for once?"

"Decent human beings will enjoy seeing news like this, believe me!" Brett walked toward the water, his phone capturing all the excitement. His brother went to the bike rack and took a soda from his backpack.

Which gave Artemis an idea.

When the boys were busy on the beach, she let the air out of the back tires of both bikes. She made her getaway toward the front entrance of the hotel, but something moving near the storage shed caught her eye.

Art pivoted and snuck around back of the shed, where Mrs. Moonchaser was seated on an overturned apple basket, peeking out at the commotion. "What are you doing back here?" Art asked.

Mrs. Moonchaser wiped her eye with the sleeve of her blouse. "Heartbreaking. This behavior is heartbreaking, and I'm not sure what to do about it."

Artemis sat next to her, cross-legged on the ground. "It's

all because of my posters. Not the peaceful attention I was going for."

"People are responsible for their own actions. Your actions were well-intentioned. Matter of fact, I heard two teenage cashiers at Dwyer's Drug Store saying they'd like a poster to hang in their bedrooms. They got a kick out of the one with two fireflies wearing sunglasses having a conversation about how streetlamps and other outdoor lights were not conducive to producing offspring. Sounds like a peaceful reaction to me."

"I suppose."

"Change comes in small steps."

They watched as the Barlow twins approached the bike rack, grinning like they'd won the lottery. "This is gonna be awesome, Henry! Maybe Channel 8 News will want our footage!"

"We're gonna be famous!" Henry said, as he unlocked his bike.

They hopped on their bikes, but their smiles melted when their rear tires went flat as pancakes.

"No way! Did we run over glass?"

Henry frowned. "It's possible. Look at all this trash around here."

Walking their bikes, they left the parking lot, their faces red with confusion.

Artemis put her hand over her mouth to stifle a giggle.

"Come on, child. Let's get out of here while the getting's good," Mrs. Moonchaser said, rising to her feet.

"This could make life worse for a lot of p-people. Including me," Artemis said. "If Mom or Mr. Hellander find out I had anything to do with this negative publicity—"

"You did nothing negative."

"I love the hotel, but I also love RT and the Sound and the salt marsh."

"That's all quite positive."

"I suppose." Artemis pointed to Agnes. "I spread compost under Agnes and all this mint sprouted. I don't get it."

Mrs. Moonchaser picked a sprig and inhaled. "Ah yes. Mint will take over a garden if you let it."

"Well, I need to do something before Mr. Hellander complains, or pulls it all up. Agnes does seem to like it. Her leaves are less droopy."

"Mint makes for some delightful tea, over-the-moon delish." Mrs. Moonchaser nibbled at the leaf. "This crop will make an ocean's worth of mint tea."

Art closed her eyes. "Just picture it, mint growing all over the hotel lawns, and people can't pick it fast enough. Maybe it smothers other plants, climbs up the hotel walls and into guest room windows—"

Ding-ding-ding! A perfect poster scenario. A case of "Too Much of a Good Thing."

"You'll figure out how to rein it in," Mrs. Moonchaser said.

"I'll pick some for Chef Paul. You help yourself too."

They each gathered a bouquet of mint.

"Smile!" They turned around to see Jess standing there, holding her camera to her eye. "I like the look of this calm scene in the middle of the jellyfish storm," Jess said.

Art and Mrs. Moonchaser raised their bouquets for the camera.

"I'm glad someone's interested in recording positive happenings at the hotel today," Art said.

"It was your poster, wasn't it, that did this?" Jess asked, pointing to the parking lot that finally appeared slightly less congested.

Art nodded. "And I'm not too proud of it."

"What do you mean? If this news gets into the right hands, it could be a big help to The Sound Seekers Brigade," Jess said.

"It's already in the wrong hands of the Barlow twins. Have you taken many other photos of all this chaos?" Jess showed Art the pictures on her phone. "Wow, these are great, Jess. But would you mind keeping them to yourself for a while?"

"Sure."

"I don't want any more negative stuff coming out about the hotel right now." Art handed her the bouquet. "Do you like mint?"

"Of course. My dad uses it in recipes all the time."

"Let's pick some more for him then." Art squatted and gathered more bouquets.

"It is awful pretty," Jess said. "You could sell it, you know."

Art examined the bunch in her hand. "You've got a point. I could tie it in bunches and fasten tags to them with recipes. The money could help the salt marsh big-time. We could research ways to restore the grasses. Or build benches where people could rest or bird-watch. Maybe even build some bird boxes!"

"The antiques fair is coming up. You could get a booth."

"*We* could get a booth?" Art raised her eyebrows at Jess.

"Sure, I'll come. I could display some of my photos of the beach and salt marsh when they were in good shape, along with the mint."

"It'd be a great way to advertise The Sound Seekers Brigade. Let's do it!"

Mrs. Moonchaser gave two thumbs-up and walked home.

Art had a change of heart. Her plan would be the opposite of war. Her plan was a proposition for peace.

15

"Artemis, you take Edelweiss, and I'll clean Morning Glory," her mother said. "They're empty. Two more families have cut their vacations short."

"Got it." Art picked up the vacuum cleaner. "Um, you think business will pick back up again soon?"

"Harry's discounted the room rate, so hopefully that'll draw more guests. But we can't afford any more bad press." Her mother eyed the *Horizons Sentinel* on the table.

Art picked up the paper. Her jellyfish poster gazed back at her from the front page. The Barlow Twins. "Wow."

"Wow is right," Mom said. "Moonchaser could be sued for defamation. Harry's profits are declining as a direct result of her protests."

"You n-never know. All this publicity will bring more attention to the hotel but maybe it'll end up being a good thing. Look how many p-people showed up in that bus wanting to see the beach." Artemis seethed at the thought of hordes of noisy litterers.

Her mother threw her hands in the air. "Please. We don't need a replay of that parking-lot fiasco. We need…Who knows what we need." She strode off down the hall with her bucket and mop swinging at her side.

Art quickly cleaned out Edelweiss and then went downstairs to the kitchen.

"Psst! Jess, can I speak to you?"

Jess wiped her wet hands on a towel. "What's up?"

"Everyone thinks Mrs. Moonchaser made those posters, and I can't let her take the blame any longer."

"You're going to confess?"

"I think I should. It's the right thing to do."

"Okay. You want me to go with you?"

Art nodded. "Thanks. Come on."

The girls headed to Morning Glory, but noise from the lobby drew them there instead.

"Don't deny it! You're the only one who is anti-hotel around here." Mr. Hellander glared at Mrs. Moonchaser, who held Prisbrey's leash in her hand.

"My dog darted away when she heard the uproar in the parking lot. She didn't trample your flowers on purpose, for goodness' sake."

"And how do you explain the posters?" Mr. Hellander asked.

"Those posters were not anti-hotel," she responded. "If anything, they were promoting good will for the land this hotel stands on."

Artemis stepped forward. "It was m-me. I made the posters."

Jess stepped up next to Artemis. "It was both of us."

Mrs. Moonchaser put her arms over the girls' shoulders. "All three of us are seeking to launch stewardship for Long Island Sound. That's what all this is about."

Mr. Hellander gave them the evil eye.

"Look, I d-didn't want to make problems for the hotel," Art said. "But since it looks like the posters c-caused confusion, I'm willing to do whatever you want to help get guests back. I c-can make new posters advertising the new reduced room rates."

"Don't even think of it. Everything you touch turns bad." Mr. Hellander spun around and went into his office.

The three Sound Seekers exited the hotel.

"Thanks, you two, but it really wasn't necessary to take the b-blame with me," Artemis said.

"Strength in numbers," Mrs. Moonchaser said.

"No way would I let a team member go it alone," Jess said. "Remember what Mr. Hyde says—"

Art laughed. "Oh, don't say it! Our gym teacher must be a hundred years old, and so is that slogan."

Mrs. Moonchaser stopped walking and turned to face them. "There is no *I* in team?"

Jess and Art looked at each other and plugged their ears. Mrs. Moonchaser smiled and went to find Prisbrey.

16

The next day, Art rode her bike to the antiques fair. She figured it would be her last outing for a while. Once Mr. Hellander told her mom about the posters, she was sure she'd be grounded for life.

The fair was a popular event held on the town green every year, and she usually went with Warren. He loved all the old tools and fishing gear, and Art always hunted for bottles for her collection. This year, she had other things on her list, too, like cast-offs to add to her collection of recycled art components. Along with wind chimes, she and the Sound Seekers would create some cool sculptures, just as Mrs. Moonchaser had taught her, to honor the shoreline. Money from the sales could be used to do whatever was necessary to help the salt marsh.

She slid her bike into the metal rack and pulled the chain lock through the front wheel, tugging on it to be sure it was secure. Turning to go, movement from the other end of the rack caught her eye. The wind played with a small fish kite tied to the seat of an orange bike. Warren's. They hadn't spoken since their earlier argument on the beach. Oh well, she'd have to face him again sometime.

But first she needed to check in with Jess at their mint booth. Propped up on the table stood a poster they'd drawn showing the benefits of mint when used in baths, as digestive aids, as potent energy boosters for athletes, and even as natural deodorizers. The girls had bunched the mint into bouquets, tied them with yarn, and attached tags that said "Save the Sound" on one side, with a mint recipe on the other. "Save the Sound" was a great motto, but it also happened to be the name of an important local nonprofit organization that stood for everything the Sound Seekers Brigade believed in. Art wanted to draw a map of the salt marsh and come up with a plan for placement of new cordgrass plantings. But she needed to consult professionals for such a big idea, and Save the Sound could help her figure all that out. Her team was growing bigger by the day.

Art took a map from the pile on the table at the entrance and zeroed in on tent number ten, antique glass works. Their mint booth was stationed outside that tent and Jess had gotten there early to open up. It was perfect, situated under a huge tree so it wouldn't be anywhere near as hot as inside a tent.

"Hey! Hey, Artemis!"

Warren waved at her from the food tent area.

"C'mon over and eat!" He raised a burrito in the air. "Just as good as last year."

It was as if they'd never argued. Art held up her index finger and yelled, "One minute!"

Jess had already sold four bunches of mint, and the fair had just opened.

"Great job, Jess. I'm going to get a burrito with Warren, then I'll bring one to you so you can have a break." Jess nodded and started a conversation with a woman who wanted to know how mint might improve her marathon time.

Artemis walked over to a tall man in a western hat and cowboy boots who was there every year and bought a burrito from him. Then she joined Warren in the shade of an elm tree. "What's in there?" she said, pointing to an oversized bag at his side.

Warren put his plate down and took a swig of lemonade. "Here. I'll show ya." He reached in the bag and pulled out a pair of binoculars. "The guy gave me these for two dollars because they don't focus right anymore. But I still think they're cool." He held them up to his eyes and looked at Artemis.

Art held out her hand. "Can I try?" She looked through the lenses and adjusted the vision. "I can see fine with these things." She scanned the area. The book tent was crowded with kids and their parents. The man with the double-sized tent of old tools and instruments was demonstrating how to use an abacus to a girl her age. The antique glass tent looked quiet, and their mint bouquets had dwindled to a dozen.

Art focused the binoculars on the book tent again. "What the—?" She adjusted the lenses just to be sure.

"What's so interesting?" Warren wiped salsa from the corner of his lip with the back of his hand.

"My father." She zoomed in on her dad with the binoculars as he entered a tent that was hard to classify. Eclectic. Odds and ends. "What's he doing here? I don't want to argue about speech therapy today."

She handed the binoculars back to Warren. He held them up to his eyes. He squinted and focused the lenses. "I see nothin'. Nothin' but blurry tents."

Art balled up her napkin and walked toward a garbage can. Bees swarmed above the rim, so she threw it in from a few feet away.

"Nice, Art! Two points."

She picked up her backpack. "I gotta go."

"Wait! I didn't show you the best thing of all." Warren rummaged around in his bag and pulled out what looked like a monster-sized pair of metal tweezers.

Art laughed. "A dentist's tool? Planning an extraction? On a rhino?"

"Fireplace tongs. You know, for moving logs around."

She pulled on her backpack. "Just what I always wanted."

"It's for my ancient tool collection. These are classics!"

"They aren't ancient, Warren. But congratulations anyway."

"Okay, old. They must be worth somethin' if they're still hangin' around, right?"

Art looked at him and considered his logic.

"Or they woulda been thrown out by now, I mean."

"Right," Art said. "Things left behind." Clouds crept around the sun, frizzling the edges like a fried egg. "Left behind, like ghosts."

Warren stuck his fingers in the handles of the tongs and snapped them open and closed like an old metal mouth. "Bruuuu-ha-ha-ha!" He swooped them up and down in front of Art's face. She pushed them away and turned to go.

"You scared of an old pair of tongs?" He swooped them around again. "I won't hurt you, I promise," he said in a high-pitched, spooky voice.

"Warren, you're the one afraid of ghosts, so quit m-making fun of me. Can't you ever be serious?"

He put the tongs back in the bag. "Can't you ever be less serious?" Art stared at him. "You hardly smile anymore," he said.

She observed him, her oldest friend, with new eyes. He was almost as tall as she was now; his hair was much longer, too, but other than those physical changes, he was the same boy who'd saved her from a couple of bully girls on the kickball field back in first grade. *Was it him or me who'd gone and changed on the inside?*

Art walked away. "I gotta go check in with Jess and our mint booth."

Warren followed her. "Wait up. I'll go with you. Make sure the ghosts don't follow you around." He smirked.

Art stopped short and stood nose to nose with Warren. "I AM SO S-SICK OF YOUR S-STUPID JOKES," she snapped, and she pushed him away. He stumbled and fell onto his back, legs in the air like a dead bug.

A man with straggly gray hair and a bald spot pointed at Art with his cane. "Easy does it, young lady." He wore a

T-shirt that said "Red Stone Landscaping: Leave your weed needs to us."

Art glared at him and then back at Warren, whose face was red and his eyes fiery.

"I've had it, Artemis!" he yelled. "If you don't want me around, then I'm outta here." He stood and brushed himself off. "The tide's comin' in. At least the fish won't yell at me for catchin' 'em." He headed toward the bike rack.

Warren never yelled. And he had never spoken to her like that before. Ever.

Art shook her fist at him. "I hope the t-tide s-swallows you up whole!" She yanked at her backpack straps as if they'd open a parachute in time for a graceful landing. The old man was still shaking his head and waving his cane back and forth at her like a cautioning finger.

My big mouth. Why was it that people always heard the words I wished I could take back, but not the ones I hoped everyone would pay attention to?

A roll of thunder and a few raindrops brought Art back. At their booth, she and Jess counted their money. "We made more than fifty dollars," Jess said.

"And there's more mint around Agnes if we need it." Artemis headed for the bike rack. "Thanks, Jess. See you back at the hotel."

"My dad can drive you home, Art," Jess said. "It's gonna storm."

"I'm fine. Thanks though."

Art unlocked her bike and hopped on.

"Never thought I'd run into you here," her father said.

"D-Dad!" She steadied herself with the bike's handlebars.

"You okay?" he asked.

"Fine."

"Why were you yelling at that man with the cane?"

"I wasn't. It was Warren."

"A little trouble in paradise?" She rolled her eyes and fingered the coins in her pocket. "But you're such good friends," he said.

"We were."

"Old friendships get strained sometimes."

"He's n-not the same k-kid. He's—"

"Shh. Slow down and take your time."

"Let me f-finish!"

"Just try your hardest," her father said.

"It d-doesn't work that way. I'll never change." She spun the bike pedal with the toe of her sandal, making it go faster and faster.

"Remember when we used to come to this fair? You were about as tall as my knee when I first brought you." She blinked twice and cleared her throat. Those were the easy days. "This is where we'd hunt for bottles for your collection. How many do you have now? That is, if you still have them."

"Thirty-two."

"Blue?"

"Six of them." She stopped the pedal and put both feet on the ground. "I g-got to go."

"You sure? We could check out the antique glass tent. And I'm on a hunt for a beaded Greek handbag."

Great. He has a girlfriend.

"Not really my style," he joked. "I just want to study the design up close. They're full of color, and I've got a client who's looking for a Greek motif to stencil on her kitchen walls. An old kitchen, but she likes it that way. I must admit it's interesting."

"Cool. But I gotta get back now." She pushed her bike onto the road.

"Okay, but don't forget we're meeting Mrs. Lundquist in the lobby at noon tomorrow."

"What? I t-told you I'm not d-doing therapy!" She hopped on her bike.

"Attitude is everything, Artemis," he called. "You know that."

A lump in her throat blocked any words she might have said. She spat into the dirt and high-tailed it home.

17

The rain pelted her bare arms. It stung like a zillion bees, but Artemis made it home from the antiques fair in a record eleven minutes. She parked her bike and squeezed water from the bottom of her T-shirt. The bad weather left her with only one option for the afternoon. Carrying out her mother's order to clean up and organize the library would be a perfect distraction from her muddled life.

Art wiped off the windowsills, stopping every so often, mesmerized by the rain streaming down the library windows. Outside, a gull braved the weather, swooping low, diving for fish, but he came up empty-beaked every time.

Next, she sprayed some organic lemon oil on a washcloth to clean the desk. If she got these chores done first, maybe it'd clear up in time to get to the salt marsh. After several days of no raking, she feared it wouldn't be pretty.

Art saved the bookshelves for last. First she'd dust, then alphabetize. She also needed to come up with a storage plan for the really old books, since there was no way she'd throw them out like Mr. Hellander wanted. She was running out of room in her closet, but the idea of recycling old books intrigued her. How could she transform them?

A rumble of thunder and a lightning flash drew Art back to the window.

"What?"

There was Warren, fishing pole over his shoulder, windbreaker hood up, walking down the dock. Art watched his familiar movements as he baited, cast, and reeled in. Then, nothing on the hook, he rebaited.

After at least a dozen casts, Warren sat down on the dock,

setting his rod beside him. He stared out across the Sound as Art stared out at him. Which made her wonder if someone was staring out at her as she stared at Warren who stared out over the Sound—like nested dolls, the wooden ones that open up revealing a smaller version of themselves. The simple truth was that if anyone was watching Artemis, it was probably the ghosts, wondering what was taking her so long to figure out how to do what she needed to do.

The drumming rain silenced her thoughts. She tapped on the pane, knowing Warren wouldn't hear her, and she wished things between them were back to normal. Rivulets streamed down the glass and distorted the landscape behind it. Life was blurred out as if by a pencil eraser, smudged beyond recognition. Art put her nose right up to the window, but her breath fogged it up. She cleared the glass with her hand.

The dock was empty. Warren was nowhere to be seen.

She moved to another window to get a better view. Nope. He was gone, and so was his fishing rod. But he couldn't have walked—or run—out of her vision in those few seconds it took her to clear the fog from the pane. She put down the rag and ran outside.

The wind blew the rain sideways, and her wet hair whipped her cheeks. She called out for Warren, running up and down the dock, peering over the edge to see if there was any evidence of him in the water. If he'd fallen in, the water was plenty warm enough for him to easily swim to shore. He was a decent swimmer.

Nothing. The words she'd shouted at him at the antiques fair spun around in her mind. "I hope the tide swallows you up whole." Were her words predicting life just like her poster seemed to have done?

She gave up the search when her shirt and shorts morphed into a second skin. Her teeth threatened to chatter right out of her mouth. Maybe Warren went home, and she hadn't noticed him leaving.

"Please, Mother Nature, let Warren be safe!" she called up to the seething sky.

She stumbled through the parking lot. The tide had come way up, edging close to the pavement. She bent over to pick up a plastic bottle and a deflated Mylar balloon. A few steps later, a plastic comb minus several teeth, and a potato-chip bag. Then, after another step, what looked like a mass of brown seaweed lapped at her ankles. She nudged it away, but then snatched it up and shook it off. Warren's windbreaker! She ran down the road toward his house with it hanging by her side like a drowned kite.

"I promise to be nicer if you just let Warren live through this!" she called out to the sky again.

The waves crested higher and higher, finally reaching the road. This was the highest tide she'd ever seen, and it wasn't even a full moon. The poor salt marsh had become so weak that it wasn't able to help hold the tide back. It would take too long to get to Warren's house, so she ran to Mrs. Moonchaser's to call 911.

Mrs. Moonchaser opened her door just as Art raised her fist to knock, as if she'd known Art was coming. "Come in, child, before you're whisked away." She tugged Art's arm and shut the door behind her. Simon held a battered flowered umbrella in his hand, obviously a rescue from a local garbage can. His head tipped toward the sky in wonder.

"P-Please, you've got to call 911! Warren is m-missing!"

Just then, the room lit up with a lightning flash, and silence fell soft and warm through the skylight. Then, unbelievably, the sun streamed through the skylight and onto Simon, sparkling him like a million fireflies. Artemis swore she saw him smile. New England weather was known to change from sun to rain and back again in minutes, but this abrupt transition from such a powerful storm to bright sunshine was very odd.

Mrs. Moonchaser opened the front door and Prisbrey

trotted out into the sunshine, her nose in the air as if picking up a scent. "I'll call 911," she said. "You'd better be on your way."

No time to waste with wondering. Art hugged Mrs. Moonchaser and bolted out the door.

"E-oh-lay. E-oh-lay!" It was RT! She listened and followed her wood-thrush friend's song.

Artemis looked closely as she picked her way through the sodden thicket at the edge of the lawn and back through the wooded area behind the hotel. All of a sudden RT changed his call. "Bup-bup-bup!" He got louder and more agitated till he shot out, "Pit-pit-pit! Pit-pit-pit!"

RT continued his alarm as Art searched through the trees and behind bushes. "Where, RT? Where is Warren?" She stepped around a cluster of rhododendrons, and the thrush went silent. Warren had to be nearby. Art examined every inch of the ground. The sun's heat drew steam from the moisture, as if every plant were cooling off after a hot bath. She scrambled through the trees and in her haste nearly tripped and fell into a big hole in the ground.

Warren lay at the bottom, muddy and wet.

"Warren! Are you okay?" Art called.

He didn't move. His fishing pole lay next to him, and he'd lost one of his sneakers in the fall.

"Warren!" Art looked around and threw up her hands. "Warren, I'm g-going to get help." And she ran back toward the hotel, pleading with Mother Nature and any available ghosts, gods, or goddesses for her friend to be okay.

By the time the ambulance and fire department arrived, a crowd had gathered, shouting encouragement to Warren. After what seemed like hours, four men and two women coordinated their efforts and hoisted him up using ladders and pulleys. He looked blue in the face, alive but only semi-conscious, his leg twisted awkwardly beneath him. The paramedics carried him away on a gurney. Artemis trotted alongside, telling him he'd be okay, whispering she was sorry for yelling at him at the antiques fair. At the hotel parking lot, they loaded Warren into an ambulance and sped away.

The crowd walked back to the hotel, murmuring and shaking their heads.

"That's what you call a sinkhole!" Mrs. Moonchaser pointed an accusing finger at Harry Hellander. "If you hadn't assaulted this earth and stressed it out with all your renovations and upgrades, this would never have happened."

"It was just an unavoidable accident," Mr. Hellander protested.

Mrs. Moonchaser faced the crowd. "This hotel has outgrown the land, and the land has responded in the only way it knows how—by breaking down. If you'd only paid attention to the clues!"

"It's all m-my fault," Art muttered, staring down at her filthy feet.

Mrs. Moonchaser stopped in her tracks. "Oh no, you don't. You were the one who saved him."

"No. I m-mean that I should have worked harder to get people to p-pay attention." Art dug at the saturated grass with her foot. "It was my privilege and my d-duty, like Rachel Carson said, to speak up about s-something so important, and I mucked it up big-time."

"Oh, there you are, Artemis." Art's mother turned to Mrs. Moonchaser. "Stay away from my daughter," she said, her eyes so hot they could've ignited a barbecue grill.

Mom took Art's hand, leaned toward her ear and whispered, "The police would like a word with you."

Skulking along behind her mom, she looked back over her shoulder at Mrs. Moonchaser, whose ear flushed fuchsia.

The policewoman held out her hand. "I'm Officer Conch. I hear you're the one who found Warren."

Art nodded and shook her hand.

"Would you tell me about it?" the officer asked.

"W-well, I followed my wood thrush's c-call and—"

"Your wood thrush's call?" Officer Conch jotted down notes on her pad. "What do you mean by that?"

Art fidgeted with the hem of her wet shirt. "The wood thrush, a b-bird I know, called me to the w-woods." A nearby policeman squinted his eyes, looked at the man next to him, and shrugged.

Crazy girl again. Focus.

"As I g-got closer, the thrush kept calling out to me." The policeman folded his arms and teetered back and forth on his heels. "T-Till he went silent. Then I knew Warren was close by. Then…"

"Then?" The policewoman raised her eyebrows.

"I-I…um…I…"

"There you are, Artemis." Her father moved through the crowd and put his arm around her. "You okay?" he asked.

She nodded.

"Mr. Sparke, I need to ask your daughter a few more questions because she was the first on the scene. Would you and your wife mind giving us a couple minutes?"

He backed up. "Of course." But her mother stood strong. Officer Conch pulled Art gently away from the crowd.

"You were saying, Artemis?"

Art's eyes darted all around the crowd and the hotel grounds. When she looked up, RT was circling the area. Art's eyes blurred and her throat closed up. *Just let me be done with this. I want to run away to a place where nobody knows me.*

"Take it easy, now, take it slow," Officer Conch said. "How about we go sit on the terrace."

Art coughed and held her hand to her throat. Her eyes watered and turned pink. A fireman who was just getting ready to leave gave her a bottle of water. "You're probably dehydrated. To say nothing of the stress you just went through," he said. Art nodded and chugged down the water.

"None of this is your fault, Artemis," her mother called, as she looked nervously around at the crowd that had dwindled to a handful of people. "Just tell the officer the truth." Officer Conch glared at Mom. "What did you do when you saw Warren lying in the sinkhole?" Officer Conch persisted.

Just then, a large man exploded from the door of the hotel. He zig-zagged across the lawn. "Well, there you are," Mr. Lowe bellowed and pointed at Artemis. "Just what esackly happened to my son?" he hissed.

Art stepped back and two policemen placed themselves on either side of Mr. Lowe. "You need to go take a seat, sir. We're interviewing a witness."

"Yer interviewin' a problem, that's what yer doin'." Mr. Lowe's face puffed up. His eyes bugged out like a beached fish. The policemen took him by the arms and escorted him to a bench.

"Have a seat." They gently pushed Mr. Lowe down to sit. "And no more liquor."

"That girl gotta temper like a demon, I tell ya," he yelled. "She pushed my boy into that stinkin' sinkhole." He wiggled out from under the officer's hand. "Aks her about why she yelled at my kid on the beach the other day. Ole Mike the fisherman told me. She got so mad she pushed Warren, I tell ya." Mr. Lowe stood up and wobbled. The policeman got a hold of Lowe's arm and sat him back down on the bench. The big guy continued to sputter.

Officer Conch looked at Art. "Is any of what he says true?"

Art's brain throbbed deep inside like a woodpecker hammering, *Rat-a-tat-tat, you're a rat.* Mr. Lowe now shouted obscenities, and her parents whispered on the front walk.

"Artemis?" The officer leaned down and looked into her eyes.

She shook her head and opened her mouth to speak. Her

lips moved but not a sound materialized. Art coughed into her hand and cleared her throat. She opened her mouth to speak again, but nothing more than a whoosh of air came out.

She no longer spoke broken words.

She couldn't speak at all.

18

Artemis rubbed her eyes. The light in the living room stung. Her father was fuzzy. She looked over at her mother. Her features finally settled into focus. Her dad offered her a glass of apple juice. "Drink something. You're just overtired." Art shook her head and fell into the fat brown sofa pillows.

"Artemis, is there something you need to tell us?" Her mother sat down next to her. "Anything we need to know?"

Art folded her arms and sank deeper into the pillows. Three cheeseburgers and a plate of fries sat in the middle of the coffee table, untouched, courtesy of Chef Paul and Jake. Dad fiddled with a catsup packet on the verge of bursting. Not exactly the time for a family dinner.

Her mother cut a burger in half and handed it to her. "You'll feel better if you eat." Art pushed the food away; the smell made her stomach churn. "At least try to help out here. Your friend is lying in a hospital bed right now, heavily sedated."

Artemis began to cry. Her mind spun with *if onlys*.

Dad handed her a napkin. She blew her nose on it and winced.

"What did Arthur Lowe mean?" he demanded.

"Garrett! Stop."

"We need to know the truth, Ellen." He turned to his daughter. "You lied to us about the posters."

I never said I didn't make them. I just didn't say I did.

All these accusations stirred up guilt and anger, even though she knew she hadn't pushed Warren into the hole. Anger won out and she stood, fists clenched, aching to land a punch. Mom sat frozen. Dad's catsup pack exploded, squirting his shirt with red streams of stickiness. Then in one clean swipe, Art hurled everything off the table. Cheeseburgers landed open-faced on the sisal rug, leaving greasy splotches everywhere. Pickles and fries scattered. Juice and red wine comingled into a fizzy, bloody concoction that dripped from the table to the floor.

Artemis stampeded through the mess to her bedroom where she crawled under the bedcovers with her rock-a-bye pillow. Her parents' rants strained at the walls, ready to batter right through them. Art put her pillow over her head and repeated over and over in her mind, "I'm sorry, Warren. I'm so, so sorry."

A knock nudged her from a semi-sleep, the place where you're just dangling, still part of the waking world, but nearly ready to drop into a dream. She dragged herself up and opened the door to find Officer Conch flanked on either side by her parents.

"Artemis, I have a few more questions for you." She took out her notebook and pencil, tapping the eraser on the page as she continued. "Your parents say you still won't talk."

Art shook her head vehemently and held out her hand, asking for the officer's paper and pencil. She wrote, *I can't talk*, and underlined the word *can't* three times.

Officer Conch read it, cocked her head, and wrinkled her brow. "You did a great job talking to me earlier. What happened?" Art shrugged. "Artemis, did you happen to see Warren fall into the sinkhole?"

Art wrote furiously. *No!*

"Did you have a fight with Warren recently?"

Art looked down, scribbling curlicues along the edge of the paper. She wasn't about to lie, but she also wasn't going to implicate herself either. Her mom piped up, "Just tell the truth, Artemis. The truth will never get you into trouble."

Art continued to scribble. Officer Conch held out her hand, and Art returned the pad and pencil. The officer adjusted her belt and put her hands in her pockets. "It'd do you good to talk about what happened. You don't want people jumping to conclusions." Art sat down on her bed, turned her back to the adults. "Okay. When you feel like talking, give me a call." The officer thanked her parents and left.

The police cruiser started up and crunched its way over the sand and pebble-strewn road. Art's parents' stares seared into her back.

Nobody will believe me even if I could talk. Nobody's on my side except Mrs. Moonchaser, but nobody will believe her either. My world's falling apart, and I'm not even sure I want it put back together again.

She walked over to her parents, put her hands on their shoulders and escorted them out of her room. Her father put his hand on Art's, then took it way. She closed the door behind them, then lay back down on her bed and sobbed. The loneliness was suffocating, and her breath came in jigjags.

When she was all wrung out, she rolled onto her side and stared out the window by her bed. A firefly tapped at the screen, and she touched it.

It was a gentle patter of wings, reassuring. *Nothing lasts forever*, it seemed to say. Fireflies had taught her that. Friendship had taught her that. But sometimes hard times sure felt like forever. She sat up and watched the firefly as its light beat on and off to a rhythm nobody could hear. And then it flew away.

19

A rt furiously pumped her bike up the hill that led to the hospital. A volunteer led her to Warren's room, and she gasped when she saw him. He was so skinny; he hardly made any bumps beneath the blanket. His face was the color of stale bread. She put her hand on his arm, focusing on the rise and fall of his chest. Yes, he was alive, just hanging out in some other zone.

"And who invited you here?" Mr. Lowe strode in and stood on the other side of the bed.

Art backed toward the door, bumping into the doctor as she entered the room.

"Mr. Lowe, may I speak with you for a moment in the hall?" the doctor said.

"Why, sure. 'Course you can." Mr. Lowe gave Art a snide glance and left the room.

Close one. Here was her chance. She sat in the chair next to Warren.

But the word *whisper* was not on Mr. Lowe's vocabulary list. His voice echoed through the hallway, "Now that's just a buncha baloney. His back got cut when he fell into that hole." Art put her head in her hands. "You can ask him yourself when he wakes up." The doctor whispered something. "Fine by me," Lowe bellowed. "You said he was getting stronger. Maybe he'll tell you himself tomorrow."

Artemis listened to footsteps receding down the hallway, then returned her focus to Warren. She took a deep breath in and exhaled.

"You're not welcome here." Mr. Lowe's bulk blocked the hallway light. "You're the reason he's here. I will order the nurse to keep you out of this room," he snapped, before heading back down the hallway toward the nurses' station.

Art sat back down next to Warren and held his hand. She thought of what she'd say to him if her voice worked. Then she mouthed the words:

Warren, I'm sorry I yelled at you and kicked sand at you like a toddler. Please get better. I never wanted anything bad to happen to you. Even when you didn't believe me about disappearing birds. Or ghosts.

Art pushed the hair off Warren's forehead and away from his eyes. He stirred and she drew back her hand quickly. Was that movement behind his eyes? She gripped his hand tighter. *Squeeze if you can hear me.* She watched their hands, waiting, hoping. Did his thumb twitch? She willed her thoughts to become a voice he could hear, a voice he knew was hers. She adjusted the blanket over his legs.

I'll bring you a burrito if you promise to open your eyes.

Did the right side of his mouth twitch up, trying to smile?

Please. Please get better. I'll come back soon.

Artemis left the room and walked down the corridor. She passed the doctor speaking with a man holding a clipboard.

"Those scars on his back are no accident," she said.

Art stopped and looked over her shoulder at the doctor. The man wrote something on his clipboard.

Speak up or shut up? she wondered again.

If she spoke up to help Warren, it could actually put him in worse danger with his dad. But staying silent accomplished nothing. It was the same dilemma she faced with the salt marsh, and she still had no good answer.

Art turned into the hotel driveway, and as she approached the storage shed, she found Mrs. Moonchaser headfirst in the hotel dumpster. Art tapped her on the back, and Mrs. Moonchaser bobbed back up.

"Aha! You're just the girl I was hoping to see." She brushed herself off and handed Art a bunch of wire coat hangers. "These'll come in handy for our next installment. We can fashion them into bird sculptures and perch them on those benches you want to build."

Between the half a dozen wind chimes they'd sold, and all the bunches of mint, they had enough money to buy some wood and hardware for the first bench. But before that, they needed to plant some cordgrass. Saving the salt marsh came before making a bench for it. But Art would need a voice if she was going to work with the folks at Save the Sound to make plans and enlist the help of volunteers.

Art opened her field notebook and wrote, *I can't talk*, and held her hand to her throat.

Mrs. Moonchaser placed a hand on Art's forehead. "Oh, dear! Have you come down with something?" Art shook her head. "Are your words jumbling?"

Art shrugged and wrote, *My thoughts are jumbled. But words won't come out at all.*

Mrs. Moonchaser put her arm around her. "The accident was not your fault."

Art wrote, *The police and my parents think it might be. I could be going to juvenile detention.*

"Jumping Jupiter! You'll do no such thing." Mrs. Moonchaser pointed toward the woods. "I'm sure that hole was created by putting up this parking lot and expanding the hotel. Water can't absorb into the soil anymore, and it gets rerouted, concentrates in one place, puts a lot of stress on the ground." She ducked back into the dumpster. "John Rantor and Harry Hellander are to blame."

Rantor?

Art tapped her on the shoulder and Mrs. Moonchaser bobbed back to the surface. She wrote, *Mr. Rantor's the builder my dad is using as a resource for his book on Greek architecture.*

"Well, Mr. Rantor's the one who was involved in all the hotel renovations. Oversights like this will ruin his reputation. To say nothing about the credibility of all the other historic homes in this town that he's worked on. Who knows where the next problem will arise?"

Art wrote, *If Mr. Rantor is the problem, my dad's book may not be published, and he could lose tenure.*

"Let's take this one step at a time. But we'll need to move at warp speed to sort things out."

Mrs. Moonchaser tucked the hangers in the crook of her elbow and walked past the hotel to her garden. She knelt in the dirt and scratched out some weeds with the hanger hook.

Art looked over at Agnes, way up into her branches and all the way down to her bulging roots. Mint leaned into her trunk as if protecting her. Artemis thought of how in hard times, Wangari Maathai would remind herself that no matter what others thought, she was fine just as she was, and that it was okay to be strong and to speak up. Artemis pieced together this and all the ideas of the ghostly ecologists like a quilt, and she wrapped herself up in it whenever she needed a comforting reminder.

20

Every day that Warren was in the hospital, Art did four bike loops. Zooming around and around didn't bring back her voice, but she did get some good thinking done during that time. When Warren got better, she'd ride a zillion state park trails with him, and they'd win the prize bicycle.

In the salt marsh she kept herself busy sketching plans to share with the volunteer coordinator at Save the Sound. She mapped out where they might plant native species, and also eventually place benches and eco-art. RT was conspicuously absent. His nest was still empty. But being in the salt marsh was better than being at home. Officer Conch came to the hotel almost every day. Mr. Lowe's voice blubbered in the bar every night. Her parents kept asking her questions she couldn't answer. The only things that kept her anchored were being outdoors and cleaning guest rooms. But she still couldn't speak.

One day, as she entered the salt marsh, Art stopped to examine the amaranth's leaves. They tingled and twitched under her touch. It was suffering big-time now. The two plants on either side of her were dead. Art wiped her forehead on her sleeve, then dabbed at her eyes. If she couldn't heal herself, she'd never be able to heal the amaranth.

"E-oo-lay. E-oo-lay!"

Finally!

Art scanned the area with her binoculars. She walked toward RT's song, toward the path leading into the woods.

"E-oo-lay. E-oo-lay." RT perched on the tip of a branch, high up above her. He cocked his head and nodded his beak.

"E-oo-lay. E-oo-lay." Art pointed to her throat and shrugged her shoulders. "Bup-bup-bup!" he replied.

You keep repeating yourself, RT.

He flew to a lower branch and stared at Art. She looked deep into his eyes, allowing herself to drown in those brown pools. Timid RT had taken a risk every time he sought out Artemis to apprise her of the status of the salt marsh. Their unlikely friendship had grown despite many challenges. She trusted RT, so whatever he was trying to tell her now was important.

"Pit-pit-pit. Pit-pit-pit." He circled her head and flew off, landing on a branch the next tree over. "Pit-pit-pit! Pit-pit-pit!"

She reached out her arms to him and mouthed the words *What? I just don't understand.*

RT kept up his call, and then from another tree farther in the woods came an echo, "Pit-pit-pit! Pit-pit-pit!"

Then two more voices joined in: "Who-who-who, who-who-who!" Then, "Conk-la-ree! Conk-la-ree!" The red-winged blackbirds! And several more appeared, until the salt marsh was awash with song.

Artemis beamed and raised her arms to the sky. Finally, she understood. She jumped up and down and yelled at the top of her lungs, "We're all stutterers!"

It's what Rachel Carson called nature's repeated refrains. The birds continued their conversation as Art celebrated the sound of her own words against the backdrop of their chorus. Art waved her arms, swooped and fluttered like a bird herself, lost in a dance of delight. "We're all alike!" she proclaimed. "It's just that your accents are different than mine!"

Yes, there was still some beauty left untouched in the salt marsh. It was right there in plain sight, but Art hadn't been ready to see it. RT circled around, nearly flew into Art's head, then darted away again. She watched as he careened his way toward the east edge of the salt marsh, hovered by a tuft of seagrass, and then flew high up into the air, so high up that Art lost track of him.

"Come back!" she yelled.

"Yep. I'm sorry to see that you've come back," someone responded.

Art froze, shaded her eyes, and saw Karla pouring something from a big bag into the mouth of a metal contraption. Fertilizer. Art recognized the label.

"You and your old notebook. Do you sleep with it under your pillow?" Karla dropped the empty fertilizer bag on the ground. "I hear you talking to plants and birds. You're not right in the head."

Art stepped out of the marsh and walked toward her, thinking she'd try a different approach this time. "Don't you have a d-daschund?"

"What do you care?" On cue, the dog yipped at them from the porch.

"Because that fertilizer isn't g-good for him."

The girl took two steps forward. "I'm fertilizing our lawn, our own property, not yours."

Art backed up a few steps. "What goes into the g-ground spreads."

Karla jabbed her finger at Artemis. "Off of my property."

Art backed up some more. Karla took two more steps toward her. Art took two steps back and then—*Splunk!* She tripped into the salt marsh muck and landed on her butt.

"That'll teach you to mind your own business!" Karla spat her words at Artemis and then went back to her fertilizer machine.

Art pulled herself up and brushed off the back of her shorts. Luckily, she'd just missed stepping on the weak grasses and the crab burrows. She removed her muddy sandals and stepped back onto the path. *Sprit-sprit!* Art spun around.

A quahog clam. *Click-click-click. Click-click-click!* A fiddler crab called to her, dancing in and out of its burrow. Then RT sang, "E-oo-lay. E-oo-lay!"

Their percussive voices mesmerized her, muting Karla's stinging words. The sound and familiar beat resounded deep down inside her. Nobody tried to stop RT's song or the clam's or the owl's just because it repeated. She held her hand to her neck and swallowed.

"It's true," she said aloud, more to herself than anyone else. "My voice isn't some wild thing that needs taming."

Karla had finished her work and was climbing the hill back up to her house. Artemis cupped her hands to her mouth and yelled to her, "I'm okay just as I am!"

Karla stopped and put her hands on her hips. Art smiled, waved to her, and walked away.

21

Mrs. Moonchaser!" Artemis ran straight for her neighbor's house and found her pruning roses that twisted up her mailbox post like red stripes on a candy cane.

"Something happened in the salt marsh. RT conducted an orchestra of birds, clams, and crabs, and they sang this beautiful song." She pointed to her cleared-up throat. "I'm back!"

"Slow down, child." Mrs. Moonchaser put down her sheers and tugged the brim of her sun hat down over her ears. "Now, details."

Art told her about everything, including her encounter with Karla. She shared her thoughts about the great array of voices in this world, how they may sound different but are actually all related.

"That's the power of observation for you. When you stay still and attend, then you become a part of the beauty you see."

Art nodded and smiled. Maybe in some other life Mrs. Moonchaser was a poet. Or a philosopher. Or maybe an intergalactic angel.

Artemis helped gather up the deadheaded blooms and put them in the canvas tarp. "RT has always been there for me when I needed him," she said. "Now I have to do my best to change the way people treat him, his friends, and their habitat. He was forced out of his home in the woods when developers started clearing the area. His nest in the woods by the salt marsh has been empty for too long. Now he flits around and disappears quick as a wink."

"He and his mate are probably building a new nest elsewhere."

"So unfair."

"Better for them to move than to live in peril. And the nest might still be nearby. Hopefully higher up off the ground and well hidden."

Mrs. Moonchaser tied up the corners of the tarp and pulled off her garden gloves. She picked up the bulging bundle, looked up at the sky, and sniffed. "I smell a storm winding up. Again. Mother Nature is not happy." She handed Art the tarp. "Put this in the backyard, would you?" She waddled toward her front door.

Art went to set the tarp down by the picnic table, but the path was strewn with debris.

"Oh no! Who did this?"

She knelt on the grass, surrounded by what used to be the bird sculptures she and her neighbor had created. Wire beaks and wings lay twisted and nearly unrecognizable. Hours and hours of work ruined. Art's big dream demolished.

Mrs. Moonchaser ran to her. "What in the universe...?" She put her hands on her cheeks and dropped to the ground, picked up one sculpture that had survived, and put it in her lap.

"You okay, Mrs. Moonchaser? We'll fix these up, no problem." Mrs. Moonchaser straightened the bird's tail feathers. Art reached out her arm to her neighbor. "Want some help getting up?"

"No, dear, I'll rise again. But for now, I just need to stay earthbound and let my worries wane."

Art sat and put her arm around her neighbor, but a few seconds later a voice hollered, "Right there, Johnny. All those need to be taken down."

She knew the voice. It was coming from the back of the hotel.

"If you're really okay, Mrs. Moonchaser, then I g-gotta go," Art said as she stood.

"Go. You're needed elsewhere. I'll be fine."

Art ran toward the hotel but stopped short when she saw a man in a hard hat standing at the edge of the woods—Mr. Rantor, Art assumed—holding a clipboard and chatting with Mr. Hellander. "Okay, Johnny, how soon can you start?" he asked him.

"It'll take at least a day to properly and safely remove these trees," Mr. Rantor said, as he jotted something down. "The library's a bigger deal. But I've got guys who can start on an indoor job right away."

"No! P-please d-don't!" Art yelled.

Mr. Hellander smirked. "So. The girl now speaks."

Art approached the men slowly. *I need to focus.* "Think of all the animals that live in these t-trees." She eyed the branch where RT perched during their nighttime conversations.

Mr. Hellander rolled his eyes. "Think of all the days you and the guests can spend in a brand-new swimming pool."

"What? There's n-no room for a p-pool."

"Why don't you leave that up to me and the installers," Mr. Hellander said with a stony stare.

"But trees would be b-beautiful around a pool."

Mr. Hellander excused himself and beckoned to Art to join him under the library window. He poked his finger at her face.

"Artemis. Back off," he fumed. "Our numbers are so low right now that I've got to do something." He moved out of the sun and into the shade of the oak tree. "And a spa will bring in guests even during the colder months."

"A spa?"

"We'll finally remodel that ancient library into something modern and useful. We'll offer massages, manicures, all the things that people want to enjoy when on vacation. I've got to get this hotel out of the red."

Art put her head in her hands. She was racing time to save RT and the salt marsh, but meanwhile the hotel was just going to make matters worse with this remodel.

"Harry?" Her mother walked over to them. "The man from the bank is here."

Mr. Hellander returned to Johnny and shook his hand. "Get back to me with a quote, and we'll go from there. I need your best deal." He headed back to the hotel and called over his shoulder. "Things are looking up, Ellen."

"Mom. This c-can't happen." Art looked at the old library windows, their flower boxes overflowing with peach-colored geraniums. They'd been a part of her life for a long time. The library and hotel needed to stay. And they needed to coexist with a healthy salt marsh.

"You've decided to talk again. How wonderful!" Her mother glowed with pride as if Art had aced an exam. "Thank you, dear." She looked her daughter up and down, searching for other good changes she might have overlooked.

"But a p-pool? A spa? Please, Mom, this remodel means t-trouble."

Her mother closed her eyes and shook her head wearily. "No." She backed away and folded her arms across her chest. "No, this remodel will make all the difference."

"B-But what about sinkholes?"

"That has nothing to do with this renovation."

"Doesn't Mr. Hellander care about anything but money?"

Mom put her hands on Art's shoulders, tight as vices. "Stop. If you grew up the way Harry did, you'd worry about money too. He worked so hard when he inherited this hotel from his uncle. A huge gift after years of struggle. If he ever loses it, I don't know what he'll do."

Artemis poked at a dandelion with the toe of her sandal. "I don't want him to lose the hotel. But I also d-don't want birds to lose their homes because of a s-stupid pool."

Her mother locked her down with her gaze. "End of conversation. You have gone way too far with your back talk. It is what it is." And she headed for the hotel's front entrance.

Artemis sat on the grass below the library window. A ladybug climbed onto her sandal and explored her toes. She closed her eyes and said, "Ladybug, ladybug, fly away home."

A long time ago, on a hike with her dad, he explained that you chant that rhyme when a ladybug lands on you, and you make a wish. If the bug flies away, then the wish will come true.

Art made her wish and opened her eyes. The ladybug was now navigating her ankle. She leaned over and blew on the bug gently. Within seconds, it took flight. Art wasn't sure if it counted if she nudged the bug along, but so far nature had been good to her. She only wished that she could return the favor.

22

"Art!"

His thin arms dangled from his T-shirt sleeves. Art knew Warren was going to be released soon, but she hadn't expected to see him this soon. Being outside had put some color back in his cheeks.

"Warren!" She ran to him and gave him a hug which he wiggled out of with a smile.

"Where you headed?" he asked.

"I've got to go to the salt marsh. Want to come?"

"I'm not walkin' too fast yet." She waved him on, and they walked side by side along the shore, past the beach scrub and onto the trail. "Artemis, you're so quiet. And you look like you just lost your best friend when you actually just got him back," Warren said.

She stopped. "We're still friends? You f-forgive me?"

"Forgive you? If it weren't for you, I might not be here."

"Thanks. I suppose that's another way of looking at it. And of course, I'm so glad you're better."

As they entered the salt marsh, Art examined the amaranth. Her droop was at least two inches lower than yesterday. "It's just that did you ever try really hard at something and then not get it right over and over again?" she asked.

"Sure. So did a guy named Thomas Edison," Warren said.

"At least he ended up with something to show for his failures." Art ran her hand through the amaranth branches. "Sorry," she whispered into her leaves.

"Why are you apologizing?" Warren asked.

"Mr. Hellander wants to d-demolish the library and turn it into a spa."

"What's that got to do with this plant?"

"If he builds the way he did last t-time, without thinking through issues like water drainage or how to dispose of t-toxic stuff...Well, look what happened to you. What's happening to her." She nodded at the amaranth.

"Far as I'm concerned, somethin' good actually happened to me in the hospital." Warren shuffled his feet and put his hands in his pockets. "You might think this is crazy, but I feel different now."

"G-give yourself time to heal," Art said.

"No, I mean a different kind of different." He looked at her, then picked at a fingernail. "When I was medicated and asleep all those days, a man spoke to me. A man that was like a—a ghost."

Art snapped to attention. "What did he look like?"

"Kind of short, thin. Not scary." He looked up at Artemis. "He told me to look at the big picture."

Art's mouth dropped open.

"He said to dream big. Then a woman came up behind him, all floaty-like with a colorful dress on, and water trickled from her fingers. She was all about bravery and standin' up for yourself. Pretty crazy, huh? Hey, you gotta keep this between you and me."

Art threw her arms around him. "No, not crazy!"

Warren extracted himself, looking a bit flushed. "Look, Art, I'm sorry I made fun of you about ghosts and all that. Bein' sedated was like a visit to some fantasy world. Except it felt really real."

"And I'm sorry I yelled." They walked along the muddy bank which was eerily vacant. "Why were you in the woods in that storm anyway?" she asked.

Warren stopped and looked out at the water. "I'd given up on fishin' that day when a gull swooped down right in front of me, plucked up an oyster, and took off. I swear it kept lookin' back at me." He looked down at his feet sheepishly.

"I had this idea—well, maybe it was a wish—that there was a pearl in that oyster, that the gull would drop the oyster on a rock, and it'd crack open, and there would be a valuable pearl in there. Worth so much that I could buy my mom and me a new house. A safe place. So, I followed the gull, lost sight of it, and since I was lookin' up and not down, I fell into the hole. Next thing I knew, I woke up in the hospital."

"So instead of getting a pearl, you got to meet ghosts while in a coma."

He nodded and smiled. "And when I woke up, I was alone. Except for this." He held out an old brass skeleton key. "I thought maybe it dropped outta one of the nurses' pockets. None of them claimed it." He turned it over and pointed to something etched on the back.

Art squinted to make out the initials. S.R. "It's Simon's! Simon Rodia, the ecologist. I know him!" She grabbed Warren's arm and started walking back to the hotel. "C'mon. Can I borrow that key?"

He handed it to her. "Listen, Art, I understand you better now. But that doesn't mean I can be a part of this big plan of yours. If my dad found out, well, that's a problem. I never know what he'll do."

Art nodded. "Now you're the one who needs someone to help you stand up to a bully. I wish I could be that person."

"I just need to hold on until I can figure out a plan for Mom and me that doesn't require owning a valuable pearl. Right now, Mom plays down all my dad's bad behavior."

"And she doesn't even know the worst of it, Warren. She needs to know."

"Not the time for that."

"I disagree." Artemis shook her head. "The time is now. I saw a For Rent sign above Ellie's Yarn Menagerie. You said your mom is teaching classes there now. Talk about meant to be."

Warren raised his hands like a cop stopping traffic. "I'll think on it. But for now, let's get back to what we were talking about. I'll try to help you a little, but I just have to do it quietly, under the radar."

Art had learned that quiet didn't necessarily get things done. Some issues needed to be spoken out loud, just not obnoxiously loud.

On the walk back, she explained all about her visits with the ghosts and Mrs. Moonchaser, the posters and vandalized bird sculptures, and details about the status of the hotel.

"So, what's your next step?" Warren asked.

"Something I n-need to check out in the library. You can come with me if you want."

In the lobby, they ran into Jess, who was putting out a tray of Chef Paul's cinnamon-raisin cookies for the guests, along with an urn of tea.

"Dad used the mint in the tea and cookies today, Art," she said. "Help yourself."

"No time," Art said. "Want to join us on an expedition?"

"Expedition?"

"I'm hoping it'll help me figure some things out."

"Okay, but I've got to be back in time to help Dad with dinner prep."

At the library, Art pulled at the door, but it wouldn't budge. Warren gave it a try too. Nothing.

"I told you to stay away from the library, Artemis." Mr. Hellander walked by carrying a bunch of long, rolled-up tubes of paper. "I changed the lock." At the end of the hall, he stopped to speak with an employee.

"We really need to g-get in there," Art said. The three stared at each other, willing themselves to come up with a way. "Wait! The window on the woods side of the library was open earlier today. War, you keep watch here. Jess, come with me."

Outside, Jess looked up at the window, then over her shoulders both ways.

"All clear," she said.

Art linked her hands down low like a stirrup, so Jess could boost herself up to the sill. "Go ahead, Jess, pull yourself up and in."

Art needed to use all her strength to boost her up, but Jess made it. She turned around and gave Art the thumbs-up. Art ran inside, and Jess unlocked the door and let her and Warren in.

Art removed the books, pulled out the shelves, pushed open the secret door, and wiggled her way into the secret hallway. Jess watched her, spellbound.

Art beckoned to her friends. "You are now officially welcome to visit the ghostly hallway."

"Um, really?" Jess asked. "Ghosts?"

"As I told you before, Jess, they're fine. They're part of The Sound Seekers Brigade. Trust me," Art said, grabbing her hand.

Jess followed with small shuffling steps.

"You sure we locked the library door?" Warren asked. "I'll check and then keep a watch out while you two explore."

Art nodded and waved Jess along, using her phone flashlight to lead them to the end of the hall where they came face to face with the locked door. Art took out the key, inserted it into the lock with shaky hands, and turned.

Nothing.

"What is this place?" Jess asked.

"Not sure, but it might be where the ghosts hang out."

Jess took out her phone. "Mind if I take a few photos?"

"Go ahead," Art said.

Art tried the door again and handed the key to Jess. "Here, you try."

She turned the key over and around and tried every which

way to make it fit. But it didn't. Art jiggled the knob and pushed and pushed.

"Rats. I wanted to gather the ghosts for a final pow-wow. Between the six of us, maybe we could come up with a solid plan to persuade Mr. Hellander not to build a spa."

They made their way back down the hall to the library, Art blinking hard to hold back tears.

As the three returned the last books to the shelves, the knob on the library door shook. A muffled voice said, "Does she think she owns this library? Ellen needs to discipline this child already." He pounded on the door. "Open up!" And then a muffled, "Now where did I put the darn key?"

The girls helped Warren to the window and over the sill, lowering him down gently. Then they dropped down onto the grass and sat and caught their breath. A cloud moved over the sun, and Artemis looked up. There was RT perched high up in an elm tree. He sat on his branch and twitched his head. One of the very trees Mr. Hellander wanted gone.

Beeeep! Beeeep! Beeeep!

Art leaped to her feet just as a yellow bulldozer backed up toward them.

"No!" she yelled.

The driver waved at them to move out of the way. They stood aside and watched as he parked the vehicle right under RT's tree. Then he hopped down to the ground.

"See you tomorrow," Johnny said, while Jess captured all of it with her camera.

Art crossed her arms, and the tears came. If she took all she'd learned from the ghosts and all her attempts to help RT, it'd boil down to this: Look at things with fresh eyes. Balance your words. Share your knowledge with others. Remember that there's something worth smiling about, even on dark days.

She could check all those boxes, but today something was still missing.

23

Artemis woke to scratches at her window screen. It was still dark. She pushed away the covers, shuffled over, and lifted the blind. Flashing pricks of light dotted the screen like some crazy computer message.

The fireflies!

"You're all back!" They ticked and flashed faster. She watched as the entire screen filled up. Then the fireflies gathered into a swarm, a focused wave of light, ebbing and flowing from the window toward the woods and back again, like a beckoning finger. She could just make out the creepy silhouette of the bulldozer.

"What are you saying?" She ran her fingers along the screen.

She'd never seen so many fireflies at once. A firefly's gestation period is longer than a few days. But it's possible they came back because they like moist areas to lay their eggs, and they do need darkness to attract mates, which would make this a perfect spot—when the hotel lights weren't blazing, that is.

Now the fireflies floated about a foot away from the window, a hovering cloud. They were saying something, and it looked like Morse Code which Artemis knew nothing about except that it was made up of dots and dashes. But she wasn't about to take nature's messages for granted ever again.

Art dressed quickly, grabbed her backpack off her desk, and fumbled her way through the dark to the apartment door. She turned the knob slowly and slipped out, tiptoeing down each stair and skipping over the second step from the bottom since it was a squeaker. The lights in the hotel lobby were dim, and Al, the front-desk guy who worked the night shift, sat in the back reading a newspaper. Art hunched over and snuck past the desk and out the lobby door into the night. She ran to the side of the building and stood under her bedroom window. The fireflies swooped down and draped her shoulders like a cape. They urged her along the side of the hotel until they were at the corner that stood adjacent to Mrs. Moonchaser's herb garden. The smell of mint permeated the night air.

The fireflies circled clockwise and then counterclockwise, over and over and over, like some crazy confused gear. Art examined the shrubbery along the hotel's foundation, searching for who-knew-what, the ground moist, mucking up between her bare toes.

"Pssst! Artemis!"

Her breath caught. "Warren!"

"I couldn't sleep. The wind kept callin' me and the waves, too. That sounds so crazy. But I grabbed this and came here." He held up his grandpa's old Boy Scout flashlight.

"Me too. I mean—" She pointed up. "They led me here. Now if I could only f-figure out why."

She looked around while Warren shined his light.

"Keep the light low, Warren. We don't want to wake up any of the guests. Or scare away the fireflies."

The beam fell on a burned-out patch of grass under the hotel kitchen's window, next to a rhododendron with stalky branches and curled-up leaves.

"Warren, over there."

In the center of the patch flashed one lone firefly, like the one who had visited her at her bedroom window the night she was sure there was never any such thing called happiness. They walked over to the spot, and she tested the ground with her feet.

"It's not mushy like the rest of the ground."

Just then, the sky rumbled, and rain came down in a deluge. Art kept poking at the patch of dead grass with her foot. It easily broke up into clumps, and the firefly flew back to the others.

"Look. There's something under here." On her knees, she dug with her bare hands, the fireflies flashing frantic, as Warren held the light. Finally, soaked and muddy, she sat back and looked at what she'd unearthed.

"A trapdoor!" Warren said as she reached for a notch carved into the wood. "Artemis, don't!"

Art heaved it open using both hands. A ladder led down into a dark abyss.

"I n-need your light."

"Don't go down there. Who knows what it could be."

Warren put his hand on her arm, but she swung her legs over the opening and stepped onto the first rung.

"Careful!" he said, and focused his light on the bottom rung of the ladder, then reluctantly followed Artemis down. The cloud of fireflies dropped lower, dangling a few feet above the trapdoor like an enormous lightbulb.

At the bottom, Warren worked his light over the room. It was about ten by fifteen feet, with dirt floors and walls. Art could just about touch the ceiling when she stood on tiptoe. The light followed what seemed like miles of glass jars and corked bottles on shelves that lined one entire wall. Dried-out plants hung from hooks on another wall and skeletal herb branches reached out with spindly fingers. A musty vapor hung heavy in the air, and Artemis sneezed.

Warren shone the light along the floor. Art wondered what ancient creatures' pawprints might be imprinted in the dirt.

"What is this place?" he asked, as he ran the light up and down the walls and ceiling. "A bomb shelter?"

"Or a storage area. Like they used in the old days." Art squinted and looked up at the trapdoor. The fireflies had left, and the stairs were dark. "A bit creepy, whatever it is."

His light caught a glint under the shelves. A wooden trunk with metal hinges covered with spiderwebs and dust from past centuries begged to be investigated. He pulled it out and tugged at the lid, but it was locked.

Artemis eyed the key on his belt loop. It dangled with promise. She held out her hand, and he unhooked the key and handed it to her.

It turned easily in the lock.

"Thank you, Mr. Rodia," Art whispered as she flipped open the lid.

Treasures. The trunk was packed with old photos, books, and letters. She picked up a pile of photos tied with twine. There were tons more stacks like that one. It would take hours to unpack the trunk. But she had been led there for a reason, and she had to start figuring out why.

Warren dug along the edge of the trunk to see what lay beneath the letters and photos, but the trunk was deeper than his arm could reach.

Artemis picked up a red book. The leather cover was worn smooth, and its edges were lined with thin strips of some sort of tarnished metal. The flimsy pages were nearly translucent, and they too appeared to be edged with what looked like tiny flecks of gold. She flipped a few pages and noticed that several had a day written in black ink at the top, in flowing cursive script. Just the day, no date or year.

On a Saturday near the beginning of the book, it described clear weather with a temperature of seventy degrees. Art read the page aloud.

"Lunch with Ms. Wangari Maathai was a treat for eyes and ears, despite the threat of rain. She described her admirable work in Kenya, estimating the number of trees she and her team planted there to be about 30,000. Remarkable! After lunch, we strolled the grounds, and she pointed out the Latin name of every tree we passed. An elm had a bit of blight, so she suggested an organic remedy which Sarah and I later concocted. We stored several jars of it in the root cellar." Art and War glanced at the rows of jars on the shelves. "If the tree doesn't perk back up, or should it die, Ms. Maathai advised me to plant two seedlings in its place. She's left me instructions on how to do that, just as if I, too, were one of her Kenyan Environmental Ambassadors. Alas, I would never be, as all of her ambassadors were women!"

"Who wrote that entry?" Warren asked.

Art flipped to the front of the book, looking for a title page or an author.

"No clue. But look. Here's the recipe for the remedy." Art pointed to a list of ingredients and directions about how to apply it to a diseased tree. "Maybe I can use this for Agnes, if we get out of here before the t-town decides to do away with her."

On the next page, a Thursday entry, an old stamp barely held on to the corner.

Artemis read. "It says he and Jay Norwood Darling ate a lunch of veal stew and fresh baked bread…Ding showed me the originals of some of the editorial cartoons he drew for the *Herald Tribune*. Satire, he calls them. Won several renowned prizes. He gave me one of the duck stamps he'd designed. Ding explained how the salt marsh protects the shoreline during storms, and he drew pictures of the kinds of birds who might reside nearby. I'm going to talk to the town about the importance of protecting that salt marsh. I feel a personal responsibility." Art gently touched the dry edges of the yellowing duck stamp.

Warren held the light lower, directly over the book. They examined the duck sketches taped to the book's pages. "Careful. The tape is so yellow and brittle," she warned, turning past those pages, hoping the sketches would stay protected pressed in between them.

"It can't be a coincidence that these visitors are ghosts you've met at the hotel," Warren said.

Art looked at her friend with fresh eyes. Mrs. Moonchaser always said to look for the "gift" in every challenge. Lately, she found looking for the gift to be a challenge in itself. But in Warren's case, she realized she hadn't ever really lost him.

"Maybe Mr. Hellander's uncle Theo wrote all this," Warren said. "Maybe he ate lunch with these people when they were alive."

"If my facts and math are correct, these people couldn't have been alive when Theo was alive."

"Then he ate lunch with their ghosts?"

"Can't make that assumption. This may not even be non-fiction. Maybe whoever wrote this was a fiction writer. Or maybe Theo didn't even write these entries."

"Theo's own uncle. He could've been alive when the ghosts were."

Art chewed her fingernail, a habit she'd given up years ago. The connections that were coming together made her feel like one tiny brushstroke in an oil painting, seemingly insignificant until you looked really closely and noticed how all the strokes relied on each other to form a picture.

Warren took the book from her and read the next entry to himself, then looked up at Art and smiled.

"Guess who's next?" Art covered her mouth and nodded. Warren cleared his throat and read, "Tuesday. A beautiful autumn afternoon. I gave Simon Rodia a tour of the house. He assessed the architectural design and was astounded at how well preserved it is. He was particularly enthralled with the mosaic tiling that Sarah created above the fireplace with pieces of several ceramic planters that had blown over during a storm and shattered. He also advised me about how to reinforce the porch beams and the chimney. Sage advice from a man some called crazy."

Artemis looked at that last word, and it took on a whole

new image. Instead of appearing angry and sinister, it looked intelligent and capable. With a capital C. Crazy-good.

The damp smell made Art's head ache, and she worried that the air couldn't be good for the old pages either. She flipped through the last pages, and a letter fell out. It was addressed to Harry Hellander. Artemis turned it over. "Warren, w-would it be awful if I opened this?"

"Well, it is illegal to open another person's mail."

"Just a quick peek?" She held it up to Warren's flashlight. "Just in case it's important?" Warren shrugged, and she lifted the flap and pulled out the letter. She read it silently as Warren read over her shoulder. When they finished, Art folded it up and put it back in the book, then placed the book in her backpack. "All these artifacts could help us when we get back to civilization."

Warren took out a stack of photos. He pulled at the twine tied around them, and it practically dissolved in his fingers, the pictures falling to the ground. They picked them up and made a neat stack, then sat on the edge of the trunk. The photo on top was taken at the beach. No sign of a dock. Just water and sand and a healthy swath of salt marsh. Art turned it over. "Look at this," she said. A notation in the same cursive script, in black ink, like the red book's entries.

Just then, a wide beam of light from the trap door cast moving shadows on the cellar floor.

"Enough with this relentless rain!" a man's voice exclaimed.

Warren clicked off the flashlight. "It's Mr. Hellander," he whispered.

Another beam of light darted in a frenzy up and down the stairs, back and forth.

Dripping pant legs appeared above the open door, and they held their breath. The wide beam swept the underground area and then landed on them.

"What in heck is going on down there?" Mr. Hellander

yelled. Art's teeth chattered. She wasn't sure if it was the cold or hearing the voice of the man who hated her more than anything in the world. "I could've fallen to my death," he said.

Mr. Hellander made his way down the ladder, tapping on each step before putting his full weight on it. He shone his light in their faces, and they covered their eyes. The beam slid over the walls and floor. "Who gave you permission to dig this up?" he demanded.

Warren stood. "We didn't dig it up. The rain washed away the dirt over the trap door, and we decided to check it out."

"Well, get yourselves up and out of here, and help me check out the hotel for exterior leaks. The rug outside of room 210 will probably need to be replaced. Who knows about the flooring underneath." He wiped his wet face with the bottom of his nightshirt. It had little anchors and boats all over it. "Let's go! Time to get your head out of the clouds and do something useful, young lady."

Artemis stood. "Sure. Okay. We'll b-be up in a second."

"Now! I need help now." Mr. Hellander stepped onto the bottom rung of the ladder and reached up to grasp the side rail, but the wind wailed and funneled down, pushing him off his perch. He fell, and his flashlight rolled onto the floor and blinked off. The trap door slammed closed. Mr. Hellander moaned.

The dark was thick and dank, and Art struggled to catch her breath. Warren clicked on his flashlight and pressed it into her hand. She shone it on Mr. Hellander. He sat up, wiping dirt from his hands onto his pajama bottoms. He stood and scrambled back up the ladder. "Keep the light on me while I open this thing up."

He pushed and heaved, but the door didn't budge. He tried a second time. Then a third. "Now what?" He sat on the second-to-top rung and put his head in his hands.

"We wait till morning for somebody to notice we're gone

and come save us?" Warren didn't sound too certain. Poor guy had already done time underground.

"I cannot wait until morning! I have a hotel to run. Repairs to make." He pushed on the door again with the terror of a trapped animal. "Help!" he shouted. "Someone help us out of here!" He banged on the door with his fists.

Art scanned the shelves and picked up a jar. "Look. We w-won't starve to death. Probably some pickles here and m-maybe jam."

Mr. Hellander gave her an exasperated look. "And they're probably full of bacteria. This root cellar hasn't been used in decades." He put his fingers into the cracks around the door and tried to wedge it open. "Come on! Open up." He grunted as he pushed and pushed and finally gave up.

"I can forget about the spa," he said. "I'll need to use the money to clean up the flooded area on the second floor. By the time I find the leak, the floorboards will be saturated. And dangerous."

Good. No renovations. All the better for the salt marsh.

Mr. Hellander continued to concentrate on the door, this time holding on to the side railings of the ladder and lifting his legs up so he could kick at it. A pretty athletic move for an old guy. The door didn't budge. Art bit her lip and frowned. Mr. Hellander looked like an inept spider hanging itself from its own web.

"Help!" Mr. Hellander gave three more big kicks and lost his balance, tumbling down the ladder. Again. A grown man in nautical pajamas with tears in his eyes. He rubbed his leg and sat, resting his head on his knee. "I almost lost this hotel twice before," he said. "I can't go through that again." He shook his head. "I've got to sell the place."

Art gasped. Was this good news or bad? A new owner might be more environmentally conscious. But then again, a new owner might tear down the hotel and sell off parcels of land to a developer, possibly making things much worse.

Her throat tightened. She'd never suffered from asthma before, but this had to be what it was like. She swooned, and Warren rushed to her side. The walls of the root cellar closed in on her. The chill and the dirt and the decayed-branch smell stung her nose. The glass jars twinkled in the sunlight. But wait—there was no sunlight.

Art fell to the ground, and her ears filled with a whooshing sound of air that she should've been breathing.

"Art! Art, you okay?" Warren shook her shoulder, lowering his head to her eye level.

Art coughed and opened her eyes. They both jerked back, as if the other were a ghost. Mr. Hellander stood behind them, frowning.

"You passed out there for a minute. How do you feel now?" Warren asked.

She sat up. "I'm fine." Actually, she was more than fine. Somehow the ancient air closing in on her opened her mind right up. Her head was clear, and her thoughts were sharp.

"It's no b-big deal." She stood and brushed herself off. "But what would be a big deal is if you sold this hotel." *There. I said it.*

Mr. Hellander's body stiffened. "It's the right thing to do," he said. "I'm not doing the place justice. And I need the money."

Art knew that time wasn't on her side, but perhaps the past would be. She glanced at the trunk full of history, and she knew what she had to do. Art took the red book out of her backpack and held it out to Mr. Hellander.

"Check out p-page four."

"I have no desire to read right now, obviously," he said.

Art held the book out to Warren who shook his head and pointed back to her.

Artemis closed her eyes and took a deep breath. *I'm okay just the way I am. More than okay. I'm strong enough to do this.*

Artemis opened the book. "Then I'll read it t-to you."

Warren nodded.

She turned to the entry about Wangari Maathai. It started out as a quiet telling with lots of stumbles. Mr. Hellander sighed and rolled his eyes. This was going to be tougher than she thought. Art read the entry about Ding Darling a bit louder. When she began to read about Simon Rodia, Mr. Hellander plugged his ears, then turned and made his way back up the ladder. At the top, he shook the handrails as if they could shock open the door.

"Get. Me. Out. Of. Here!" He rested his head on the top step, his back to Art and Warren, and his body shook.

Art followed him up the ladder until she was eye level with his bare feet. She'd half expected him to dismiss this evidence, so she continued on, undaunted.

"Those entries were surely written b-by your relative," she told him. "Your family was the sole owner of this property. So, your uncle, one of them, wrote this s-stuff." Her confidence grew with each elaboration.

"Pffft. You've got no proof of that," he mumbled.

Art was determined to use the entries to her advantage, regardless of the fact that she couldn't prove the book was his uncle's. She'd have to skirt around the scientific requirements of validating evidence this one time. She cleared her throat. "D-do you recognize the lunch guests in the stories?"

The silence in the root cellar could've conjured up any number of imaginary voices in its vacant air. But finally, she distinctly heard Mr. Hellander. "An environmentalist. A cartoonist. A builder. They were dead by the time my uncle Theo could've invited them to lunch." He shook his head. "And if those guests were ghosts, Uncle Theo must've had a mental problem."

"I don't think so." Time to change strategies. "Maybe it's n-not a diary at all. Maybe Theo, or your great uncle, was writing a book of fiction."

"My uncles were businessmen, not writers. And even if

they wrote, so what?" He raked his fingers through his wet hair and scratched his head.

"If one or the other entertained these ecologists, or even wrote about them in a book of fiction, it's obvious he agreed with their g-goals. How do you think your uncle would feel if he knew his b-beloved estate was being sold off to some stranger?"

"Look, whatever was going through my uncle's head when he wrote that—if he wrote it—won't change my mind about the renovations. Or about selling."

"But he g-gave the place to you. Trusted you. Left it in your capable hands."

"I tried to maintain the character of this estate. I grew up here. But the bills and the repairs. I don't want to end up destitute like my father."

Art glanced down at Warren, who furrowed his brow.

"Your uncle Theo was like a father t-to you," she said.

"Doesn't matter now. He's gone, the hotel's going down, and I'm going down with it." The wind moaned. Or maybe it was Agnes. Or RT. Or the amaranth.

Mr. Hellander looked up at the trapdoor. It creaked in the gusty air. Then it creaked again. "Oh, shut up!" he yelled. Art watched, astonished, as the man in front of her transformed into a frightened young boy. Only his graying hair and the lines around his mouth gave away his age.

There's no way the hotel's going down. Time to up the stakes.

Art placed the book on the stairs by Mr. Hellander's feet. Holding tight to the handrail, she took the envelope out of the book and held it up to Mr. Hellander. "Maybe you never g-got to read this?"

Mr. Hellander reluctantly took the envelope and scanned the enclosed letter by flashlight. His mouth twitched and he blinked fast.

"Your uncle Theo m-meant for you to read the letter that his uncle sent him," Art said. "His uncle wanted to be sure he was leaving this place to somebody who would care about his home and the land as much as he d-did. It's like he was thanking the earth for taking care of him and his wife all those years." Mr. Hellander folded the letter back up. "My aunt Sarah. She was sick a lot."

Art descended the ladder to let Mr. Hellander down. At the bottom, he surveyed the jars lined up neatly on the dusty shelves. "My uncle and I grew herbs and made tinctures that eased Aunt Sarah's symptoms." He pulled down a jar. The liquid had evaporated and a dried-up powder on the bottom of the jar billowed when he shook it.

She had one last chance. Art pulled the photo out of her back pocket and held it out to him. "L-look at this."

"Uncle Theo!" Mr. Hellander exclaimed, pointing at the man in the photo. "And that's me as a kid. That's the day we went bird-watching. He taught me how to use binoculars and identify birds using a guidebook. He's the one who taught me how to fish and sail too."

"So that's you as a kid?" Warren asked. "We thought the man in the photo was you. You look just like your uncle."

"Where did you find all this stuff?" Mr. Hellander asked, taking the photo from Art.

They showed him the trunk, and he examined each item carefully. Art estimated it had to be close to morning, and perhaps passing the time this way would help her cause.

After they unpacked much of the top layer, she caught a glimpse of an object beneath a sheaf of papers, something blue and green. She removed a few more stacks of photos and unearthed a porcelain planter. And then another, and another.

Mr. Hellander reached for one and pulled it out. "Well, I'll be darned. We planted herbs in these indoor planters so we could use them for Aunt Sarah all year round."

They lined up the three planters, each about a foot long and five inches deep. Two were unbroken, the blue, green, and white design bold and intact. But the third had been mended with glue so that there were breaks in the continuity of the design.

"There used to be five of these, all identical, according to my uncle." Mr. Hellander ran his finger over the planter's ragged edge. "A couple of them blew over in a storm, years before I was even born, and shattered completely. And this one—I dropped this one carrying it to the sink. We tried to fix it but as you can see, it probably won't hold up to heavy use."

He fingered the chain around his neck and pulled it out of his nightshirt. A pottery shard dangled from it. He unclasped the chain and held the shard up to the broken edge of the planter. It fit perfectly, a completed piece to the puzzle. "Yes. It's been a long time."

"You should k-keep them, bring them inside," Art suggested. "Put them on the kitchen windowsills. You're their rightful owner." Mr. Hellander nodded and put the necklace back on. "Just like you're the rightful owner of the hotel," she added.

Mr. Hellander picked up the red book and tucked the photo into its pages. He looked at Artemis and then back down at the book. "Uncle Theo would've liked you."

A warm glow filled Art with new feelings toward this man, whom she'd basically written off as evil.

Mr. Hellander sat on the dirt floor and read silently, while Warren and Artemis replaced the items in the trunk. "You did good, Art," Warren whispered. "Took guts to speak up like that."

"Thanks. It won't reverse all the bad stuff that happened when I couldn't speak up, but now I know I can do it. And do it well."

Warren put the photos in a neat pile and tied them up with twine. "So…I told my mom."

"You did? As of yesterday, you wanted nothing to do with that idea."

"Dad went on another rampage last night and took off in his car. When Mom assured me he'd come back like he always does, I decided it was time for her to know the truth. When I told her what he'd done to me, she cried. Then I told her about the rental in town. Mom said this was the last straw, and she called Ellie. In fifteen minutes, we'd packed some bags and were hightailin' it to her house. We're stayin' in her living room on a couple blow-up mattresses till the apartment above her is ready for new tenants. That's why I couldn't sleep tonight. The blow-up mattress must have a leak in it."

Art threw her arms around her friend. "Now you're the one who's being brave, Warren."

"Yeah. It's not over yet, but it's a start."

Pounding on the trapdoor jolted them awake.

"Artemis! Are you down there?"

"Dad! Yes! With Warren and Mr. Hellander." They all stood up and brushed themselves off. Art's knees felt creaky, and she badly wanted to make use of everything a bathroom had to offer.

The door gave a deep screech, and sunlight tumbled down the stairs, flooding the root-cellar floor. They stood at the bottom of the staircase and squinted through the dusty haze.

Her father held out his arm. Art let Mr. Hellander and Warren go up the ladder first. Then she turned and glanced again over the rows and rows of jars and the trunk, determined to commit the sight to memory. Somebody would have to come down and at least rescue the photos. So much left behind. So much to treasure.

When she finally stepped into the light, her father hugged her. "Welcome back from the depths of antiquity. You spent a night in an old root cellar, and I can't wait to hear all about it." Her mother joined the hug. "Let's let Artemis shower first before we start peppering her with questions."

Chef Paul looked on, wringing his hands on his apron, and Jess took photos left and right. "The survivors emerge unharmed!" she declared.

"We did okay, considering, didn't we?" Mr. Hellander said, looking at Artemis. A tentative smile formed on her mother's face, and it grew as the surprise sank in.

Artemis took a deep breath of fresh air. She smelled the pines in the woods, the brine of the Sound, and the sweet beach roses. What a welcome.

Beep-beep-beep! The bulldozer by the edge of the woods was backing up, and the driver lifted the blade with the hydraulic arm.

"NO!" Art screamed as she ran toward it, Warren following.

At the sight of her, Johnny Rantor shut off the engine abruptly. "Outta the way," he said. "You could get hurt." He turned the engine back on.

"Stop!" a voice yelled from behind.

Mr. Hellander ran toward them. He put his hands on his knees and tried to catch his breath. "I changed my mind, Johnny," he said. "I can't do this right now. Need to think things through."

Johnny threw up his hands and drove the bulldozer off the property.

"I say we head inside for brunch. Omelets and blueberry muffins on me," Chef Paul offered. "Warren, I called your mom and she'll be here soon."

Artemis pointed at the sky. "I almost don't want to be inside on a day like this." Just then a bird swooped low, landed on a dormer to the left of the library, and began to preen.

"Is that RT?" Warren asked.

"Nope. A red-winged blackbird. Listen to her chatter." Mr. Hellander shaded his eyes and watched the bird for a good minute. "Paul, we'll meet you in the kitchen. I need to show the kids something first."

Art looked at Warren, held up her palms, and shrugged.

"Follow me, you two," Mr. Hellander led them inside and into the library.

Artemis couldn't help wondering if he'd found out she'd been messing around with the bookshelves, but after last night, being scolded didn't feel like a possibility.

Grunting, Mr. Hellander began removing books from the shelves. Art's stomach sank and she hooked her arm with Warren's to steady his shaking. "Let's go," Mr. Hellander said as he pushed open the door and ducked through.

Art practically dragged Warren along behind Mr. Hellander as he made his way down the narrow hallway till he stopped at the locked door and knelt down. "Hopefully, it's still here." He slid his fingers under the door and fiddled with something. *Rrrrip!* He stood and held up a key. "Velcro! What an invention."

"Oh, you have got to be kidding," Art whispered.

Mr. Hellander opened the door. "Welcome to the hurricane shutter storage room." Heavy white wooden shutters were propped up against three walls. On the fourth wall, a square window was set in a dormer. Below the window stood a telescope.

"Whoa! This looks ancient!" Warren exclaimed as Mr. Hellander brushed dust off the brass tube and the walnut tripod that supported it.

"I'm really not sure how old it is. My uncle bought it for me at the antiques fair when I was about your age." He extended the tripod legs and pointed to the eyepiece. "Go ahead. Give it a go." Warren eagerly adjusted the lens and pointed the telescope at the window.

"But why keep a telescope in a locked room?" Artemis asked, disappointed that this wasn't a conference room for ghosts after all.

"I was a shy kid and preferred being behind the lens rather than playing with my cousins. The two times my father came to visit, he accused me of having my head in the clouds and never amounting to anything. The kids called me Geeky Galileo. So Uncle Theo helped me set it up here where it's more private. This became my escape room when my aunt got sick, and nurses and physical therapists kept her and my uncle busy for much of the day."

"Did you use it mostly at night?" Warren asked, keeping his eye to the lens and adjusting the focusing knob.

"All times of the day. There was always something to see."

"But why d-don't you still use this space?" Art asked. "It's so cool and guests would love to check it out."

"The hallway got closed off during a renovation because it's not usable for much with such a low ceiling."

"I'm just saying that there are plenty of guests looking for a quiet place to hang out and see nature in new way. And kids would love the secret passageway to get here."

"Hmm…Let's talk about that over brunch."

"Wait! Can I take a turn?" Art asked.

"Warren and I'll head to the kitchen," he said. "Meet us there when you're done."

As they walked back down the hall, Artemis heard Warren ask Mr. Hellander about ghosts at the hotel. His reply was, "Anything's possible." Simon Rodia would be proud.

Art pressed her eye to the telescope and adjusted the focus, then scanned the area outside the window. Artemis didn't think her appreciation for nature could get much greater, but seeing it from this vantage point proved her wrong. Bright white clouds streaked like paint across a turquoise sky, interrupted only by a canopy of green-leafed branches. She zoomed in on a dark spot in the upper branches of an oak tree situated away from the edge of the woods. "What?" She rubbed her eyes and refocused. A female wood thrush sat in a nest, and RT perched on a branch above her. "They must be working on a second brood! I can keep an eye on the hatchlings from here."

It occurred to her that Warren, Mr. Hellander, and she had spent last night incubating too. They'd hunkered down in the root cellar, and hours later they emerged, each of them changed, looking at the world with fresh eyes.

Art knew she'd visit the root cellar again. It was bursting with history. It was a place full of words waiting to be spoken.

EPILOGUE

(Reprint courtesy of the *Horizons Sentinel*)

LOCAL GIRL MAKES BIG DREAMS COME TRUE

Long Island Sound advocate Artemis Sparke and her Sound Seekers Brigade have not only managed to help restore the ailing Fiddlers Marsh area, but have also rebooted the financially troubled Horizons Hotel.

Artemis is only twelve years old.

Using funds raised from selling herbal bouquets and tin-can wind chimes (with clappers made from discarded BBs), the Sound Seekers, with the help of local nonprofit Save the Sound, planted cordgrass to fortify the salt marsh. They also donated two benches made from found driftwood and several bird sculptures created from recyclables to enhance the area around it. (See photos, page 3, courtesy of Jess Winters.)

After finding a trunk full of artifacts in an abandoned root cellar, Artemis persuaded Horizons Hotel owner, Harry Hellander, not to sell his property, which borders the salt marsh and has been owned by his family for a century. Art's father, Garret Sparke, a professor specializing in Greek architecture, offered his design services to begin updating the hotel to eco-friendly. Artemis researched and helped design an eco-pool highlighting plants and wildlife unique to our area.

"The salt marsh is as much a home to me as the hotel," Artemis says. "They've both been around for a long time, and when it seemed like I'd lose both, I knew I needed to listen to voices from the past to make sure both places survived. That probably sounds a little weird, but we can learn a lot from how people solved problems a long time ago."

Rebranding the hotel as "nature-inspired," bookings have increased, and more locals have been hired to maintain the hotel and its services. Asked about his change of heart, Mr. Hellander says, "A year ago none of this would've been possible. I can be stubborn, but Art and her gang helped me figure out how the hotel can be both profitable and eco-friendly. And it's working."

Instead of demolishing the hotel library to build a spa, chairs that unfold into massage tables are now set up around the eco-pool. Near the refurbished library is a secret passageway leading to an observation room complete with telescope, binoculars, and bird guides. Artemis and her team have spearheaded a plan for proper disposal of trash in receptacles designed to resemble schools of fish. Their neighbor, Marion Moonchaser, keeps up the gardens and manages the composting for Chef Paul's herb and vegetable gardens. Future plans include installing solar panels and restoring the abandoned root cellar which housed Hellander family artifacts.

"This hotel is full of stories," Artemis says. "The salt marshes and beaches around us have plenty to say too. We just have to listen. And then, speak up."

And that's exactly what Horizons, Connecticut, is planning to do.

AUTHOR'S NOTE

Artemis was born from my observations of my students and other children interacting with nature on our Connecticut shoreline hikes. (That's not to say that I haven't witnessed adults talking to birds and plants too!) As Artemis spent more and more time with RT and his salt marsh friends, and as she began to witness their decline, her sadness and anger got in the way of her voice, halting her words, and finally shutting down her voice completely.

Many children and adults struggle with speech. As a very shy child, I often froze when having to speak to a group, and I avoided those situations as a result. Teachers always commented that I needed to speak up in class more, but when I did, I would often forget what I wanted to say and then said nothing.

I have family members and friends who are stutterers, and Artemis came to me as a stutterer. Like me, she found solace and healing in nature. Just as there are many types of speech impediments, there are also many ways that stuttering presents itself. Many individuals helped me represent Artemis authentically, both physically and emotionally, and I'm grateful to the stutterers and therapists who took the time to help me understand Art's nuances. My hope is that all children who read her story will come away with a better understanding of those who struggle with speech, and in turn they will come to peace with their own voice however it sounds, and use it to share their story.

Having lived on the Long Island Sound shoreline most of my life, I can attest to its importance as a source for emotional and physical resiliency, learning opportunities, and just plain joy. I join many others in my concern for its longevity.

As mentioned in the book, Save the Sound is a local non-profit that has always held a place in my heart. Here's what they have to say:

Save the Sound is a nonprofit organization that protects the environment in Connecticut and New York. We fight climate change, save endangered lands, protect Long Island Sound and its rivers, and work with nature to restore ecosystems.

Unlike other businesses and companies, a nonprofit is a kind of organization whose main goal is not making money. Nonprofits instead focus on working towards the greater good for society. Save the Sound is a special type of nonprofit that works in many different ways; we are made up of environmental lawyers, scientists, and volunteers, and together, we work to restore and protect all that impacts the Long Island Sound region's environment. This means the rivers, shorelines, forests, air…you name it! For more than 40 years we have made sure that people and wildlife can enjoy the healthy, clean, and thriving environment they deserve—today and for generations to come.

www.savethesound.org

A portion of the proceeds from the sale of this book will be donated to Save the Sound.

ACKNOWLEDGEMENTS

Judith Wilcox, it is because of you that I am a writer. When I was unable to speak my own story aloud, you encouraged me to write it, and for that I'm forever grateful. You taught me the healing power of stories by kindling that very first flame that ignited my passion for writing.

Elizabeth Strazar, you unceasingly stoked that fire, and I thank you for always believing in me and my Brave Girl protagonists. The numerous hours you spent reading revisions and facilitating conversations between Artemis and me kept my imagination and confidence flowing. Your spark buoys my spirit.

Thank you, Jaynie Royal and Pam Van Dyk for offering to bring Artemis's story into the hands of young readers and helping me make it the best it can be. Regal House/Fitzroy Books is my dream come true!

Leah Andelsmith, my very first critique partner, your kind and insightful feedback and your endless brainstorming over the years has brought my writing to the next level many, many times! So grateful for your creativity and friendship.

Editors and critiquers, Kathryn Craft, Janet Morrison, Stephanie Tashman, and Angela Rydell and her Novel Salon Group: Michelle, Trix, Danielle, and Melanie, your keen eyes and wise words kept me going through numerous revisions.

Thank you, Tony Spinelli. You generously offered insights into the nature and ecology aspects of this book that made the story blossom. Your enthusiasm for the plants and creatures of our world is contagious!

To my students through the years, you demonstrated with perseverance and passion that limitless opportunities await us all regardless of individual differences and challenges. You are my inspiration.

So grateful to my sons, Nicholas and Greg, and my daughter-in-law, Jordan, for your love and sense of humor, and for demonstrating spirit and creativity in everything you pursue.

Whether clamming, camping, or hiking with Dad, or learning plant names and conversing about birds with Mom, you two defined beauty, faith, and love in a way that has settled deep down inside me. Thanks, too, to my sibs, Kirby, Janet, and Gretchen, who each in your own way remind me of what's really important.

To my dear grandson, Everett. Every time we're together you marvel at the moon and stars, whisper to the wind, and question all of nature's curiosities. May you always find joy and solace in the outdoors, and if you must be inside, may you find them in books.

And finally, thank you Chip. For decades you've selflessly devoted time, energy, and endless passion (and patience!) to me and all of my projects. So here we are again, on the threshold of something new, ready to dance in the moonlight, loving just the way we are.

RESOURCES

For information on stuttering:

Friendswhostutter.org (Friends: The National Association of Young People Who Stutter)
Stutteringhelp.org (The Stuttering Foundation)

Domestic Violence:

If ever you feel unsafe (like Warren did) or know someone who does (like Artemis did), tell a trusted adult or call: The National Domestic Violence Hotline: 1-800-799-SAFE (7233)

In addition, each state and town's website have listings of regional community resources.

For Educators:

Please see Kimberly's author website for STEAM activities, explorations, and booklists linked to *Artemis Sparke and the Sound Seekers Brigade* that may connect to your curriculum: kimberlybehrekenna.com

BOOK CLUB QUESTIONS

Conflict can appear in a story between two characters, between a character and nature, or within the character as she questions herself. Discuss the different ways that Artemis was in conflict and how they changed her way of thinking or behaving.

The three environmentalist ghosts, Wangari Maathai, Ding Darling, and Simon Rodia, all faced obstacles in their lives. What obstacles did they experience and how do they compare to Artemis's? How are they like or different from obstacles you face in your own life?

What caused Artemis to embrace her stuttering voice while in the salt marsh? Discuss the things that happened leading up to that day that might have caused her change of heart.

At the hospital, Artemis decided not to tell the doctor about Warren's father. Do you agree or disagree with her decision? Why? Have you ever been in a situation where you questioned whether to speak up? How did you decide what to do?

Artemis and Warren have ups and downs in their friendship just like we all do. If they had to create a guidebook about friendship, what is some advice that they might share? What personal advice would you add to such a guidebook?